Tainted Love

Soon to be released
By Lynette Snell

New Beginnings

Hidden Truths

Tainted Love

Lynette Snell

For Mark

The love of my life

Thank you to everyone who supported me though the seemingly endless months of work it took to get this book to print and for never wavering in their love and support.

Prologue

Carley sat on her bed with the covers drawn up around her neck. Her body tensed as she saw the headlight beams swing across her bedroom wall. The all too familiar crunch of the tyres on the gravel sounded outside. The car sat there idling for a couple of minutes, then the engine died. She heard some incoherent mumbles drift in her window as he struggled out of the car, then a loud curse as he slammed the car door shut. She waited for the sound of his keys rattling in the lock as he fumbled to open the front door. The door gave a loud creak then slammed shut again. His heavy footfalls sounded on the wooden floorboards downstairs as he made his way into the kitchen. A loud crash followed by a curse drifted up the stairs. Her eyes turned to her bedroom door. She listened intently. The house fell silent. The breath eased out of her lungs. Pushing back the covers she slipped out of bed and moved to the door. Her hand hovered over the switch as she eased the door open and stood listening for sounds from below. A footstep sounded on the stairs, then another. Her breath caught in her throat. She quietly clicked the door closed and hurriedly slipped back into bed drawing the blankets up over her head. There was no mistaking the heavy laboured breathing outside her door. She closed her eyes and pretended to be asleep. The door eased open. He stood framed in the doorway. The smell of alcohol filled the room. Drawing the blankets in tighter she wished him away. The light went off and she was suddenly engulfed in darkness.

Chapter One

Carley sat on the balcony, perched high above the city streets. Her finger idly traced the rim of her mug as she gazed out over the scene below. The early morning breeze played around her, tugging at the ends of her thin silk robe. A smile creased the corners of her lips as she watched the first rays of light filter out across the sky. Long dark shadows began to slither their way silently between the buildings and stretch out across the near deserted streets. A small contented sigh escaped her as she watched her little part of the world slowly awake from the last peaceful hours of the night. She lifted the mug, savouring the flavour as the warm liquid slowly trickled down her throat. Living in the city suited her. It was so easy to stay detached from everyone around you. People simply didn't have the time or the inclination to get to know one another and that was just how she liked it. Placing her mug back down on the table, she pushed her hand down into the pocket of her robe and pulled out a crumpled envelope. It had been delivered two days ago and still she hadn't found the courage to open it. Many times she had found herself staring down at the postmark knowing with a growing certainty that her life was about to change. A small tremor shot through her body. Why now, after all these years she wondered? Her hands began to tremble as she tore open the envelope and slid the letter out. Her eyes slowly scanned the page. When she reached the end, she simply dropped her hand and let the letter slip from her grasp. It was instantly snatched away in the breeze. Her eyes followed its path as it floated weightlessly before her, dipping and diving in the air current until finally it drifted from sight. Over the years, she hadn't let herself think about the place she used to call home. Rising to her feet she moved to the edge of the balcony. Her robe billowed out behind her as she leant forward and rested her elbows on the railing. The cool morning breeze swirled around her capturing it, and gently lifting it off her shoulders. It glided down her body catching at her elbow and settling across the small of her back. A shiver ran up the length of her body as the cool morning breeze brushed across her naked skin. Modesty was a virtue that she had been forced to dispense with years ago. Her gaze drifted across to the harbour. An early morning fog had rolled in off the sea blanketing the bay. The Golden Gate Bridge hung eerily in the mist its base now totally obscured from view. The sun's early morning rays struggled to penetrate the dense cover, throwing random golden shafts of light down on the scene. She could just make out the faint glow of headlights as the early morning traffic began its slow crawl across the bridge, fighting its way into the city hub. Her eyes moistened. This would be the last time she would look upon this scene and the thought filled her with regret. The day had finally come as she always knew it would. It was time to lay her past to rest and the only way she knew how to do that was go back to where it had all started to go wrong. A single tear trickled down her cheek. She quickly brushed it away. Now wasn't the time to open the floodgates that she had so carefully locked years ago. That lost, frightened little girl who had come here hoping to escape her pain never really had. Pushing away from the railing she dropped her arms and let her robe slip to the floor. Tossing back her long mane of dark hair, she drew in a deep sobering breath as she let the breeze sooth her troubled mind.

A noise from inside the room dragged her back to reality. Reaching down she snatched her discarded robe up from the balcony floor. As she stepped through the door her eyes moved to the bed. The occupant still appeared to be sleeping. She tiptoed silently across the room. He gave a loud groan. Her breath caught in her throat. Motionless she stood until the sound of his shallow even breathing returned. Dropping her robe on the end of the bed, she hurried into the bathroom closing the door behind her. Her reflection caught her eye and she quickly turned away. The cruel reality of what she had become, disheartened her. Reaching over she flipped the tap on and stepped into the shower letting out a small gasp as the cool water hit her skin.

She slipped the towel from the rail and hurriedly dried herself. As she entered the bedroom she stole a quick glance across at the bed. He was lying on his back, his mouth agape. Loud rasping sounds were coming from deep within his throat. Her body gave a little shudder. No matter how many men she slept with, that little wave of repulsion never went away. Her shoulders sagged as she realized that the real Carley had never had a chance. Picking up her clothes she began to dress, her eyes continually flicking to the bed. She smoothed her hands down over her rumbled clothes. Snatching up her handbag she headed back into the bathroom. Pursing her lips she applied a single coat of lipstick, the only addition to an already near perfect face. Her bag snapped shut. Moving back into the bedroom she reluctantly made her way over to the side of the bed. His assumed name was Anthony. He looked to be in his mid forties. His head was crowned with a full head of hair which was now only just starting to show a few flecks of grey at the temples. His skin was well cared for and held a slight olive tone. Her brow creased as she realised she couldn't even remember what colour his eyes were. He was in reasonably good shape for a man his age, with a strong thick chest and mildly toned abdomen. Her thoughts wandered. If she had had a different life, would she have been with a man like him? Maybe she would be the boring wife whom he was now cheating on. Her body gave an involuntary little shudder. There was no way she was ever going to subject herself to that kind of treatment. Putting her bag down on the dresser she reached in and pulled out a small note pad, a perfume bottle and a pen. Tearing off a piece of paper she gently placed it against her freshly painted lips. When she drew it away a distinct lip print remained. Lifting her perfume bottle she sprayed a light mist into the air and drew the paper through it, then picked up the pen and wrote:

"Thank you for an amazing night!!!
Monica."

"Monica" being her assumed name of course. In the twelve years she had worked in this industry she had never once used her own name. She placed the note down on the nightstand beside the bed. Dropping everything back into her bag she took one last look at the sleeping figure then left, closing the door quietly behind her.

Stepping into the waiting elevator she pushed the button for the ground floor. The doors opened into the lobby.
"See you next time" the doorman called rather sarcastically as she strode past him through the front doors.
Glancing back she simply smiled, knowing that for her there wasn't going to be a next time. Flicking her hair back over her shoulder she walked off down the street, deliberately exaggerating the sway of her hips.

A small quiver ran through her body. Knowing he would be watching; they always did.

Chapter Two

It took her just over ten minutes to walk down to the next block. Her eyes took in everything as she tried to permanently etch the scene into her memory. The letter had given her the push she had needed. It was time to move on with her life and stop hiding. There was a new feeling welling up inside her, one she hadn't felt for a very long time. Hope.

Gary's apartment was housed in one of the most expensive waterfront apartment blocks in San Francisco. The views from his window could only be described as spectacular. Huge floor to ceiling glass doors ran the full length of the building giving uninterrupted views of the city and surrounding harbour. In the summer the whole side wall could be opened up to let the city in. She had hoped to one day be able to afford one of her own. Now it no longer seemed important. What she wanted most of all was a chance at a normal life. One she felt she had been cheated out of, all those years ago.

Choosing to take the stairs instead of the lift was her way of staying in shape. She quickly made her way to the third floor. Rummaging in her bag she pulled out a set of keys, which she slipped into the lock. The door swung open and she walked in, pushing it closed behind her. If she had had a choice it would have been to never to step foot in this apartment again, but regretfully there were a few loose ends she needed to tie up before she left.

Gary looked up as she entered, a slow grin spreading across his face. "How's my favourite girl?"
"Great," she replied stiffly.
Two girls lay sprawled across the sofa. A smile rose to her lips. Rosie and Katrina were probably the closest thing to friends that she had. Ignoring Gary she made her way over to them.
"Hi you two, how's things?"
Katrina gave her a knowing wink, "oh you know, same old same old, can't complain though, the money's good."
Carley gave a soft laugh, knowing only too well she was referring to some of the older clients. For years she had made a point of keeping to herself, unable to put her trust in anybody. Then one day out of the blue the two of them had turned up looking for work. For reasons she was still unsure of she had found herself drawn to them. Now she felt she wouldn't have survived without them.

From the minute she walked in, Gary couldn't take his eyes off her. The day she had dropped into his life had been the turning point. His business had done nothing but increase in revenue since her arrival. The instant he had seen her, he knew he had to have her. So what if he had used her desperation to his own advantage? If it wasn't him then someone else surely would have. She had turned out to be one of his better investments. Back then he had been housed in a rundown apartment block in a less desirable part of town. With the income she had help generate he now lived what he considered the perfect life. To this day, she hadn't offered him any explanation as to how she had ended up living on the streets.

Her body gave an involuntary shiver. Without looking, she knew he was watching her. How naive and desperate she must have been. Like everyone else in her life he had betrayed her, but by then it had been too late to turn back. He had made damn sure that she was dependent on him for her survival. She should hate him for what he had forced her to become, but he had been a part of her life for so long now, he was the closest thing to family she had. Her eyes turned to the window as a sudden sense of loneliness washed over her. Her focus was drawn to a couple and their two children down on the wharf. It was hard to believe that she was once part of a happy loving family. Some days she felt so alone. She gave a long sigh; there was no point in dreaming of something that would never be. There was no way she would ever let herself be hurt like that again. Love was a wasted emotion that only ever caused you pain.

A glint appeared in Gary's eye. Over the years she had become his obsession. His pulse quickened as she turned to look at him. Her body went tense. Did he honestly think that she wanted to be with him? A cold shiver ran up her spine as she remembered back to her very first client. How could he have done that to her? She had only just turned sixteen and was still very naive and trusting. The client he had arranged for her was well into his forties, the same age as her father. It was on that very night that she realized that no one could be trusted. Over the years she had learnt how to disconnect herself from reality. She had erected a wall around herself and slowly withdrawn from the world.

It was the only way to protect the vulnerable little girl who had been thrown into a cruel and uncaring adult world. Drawing in a deep sobering breath she blinked back her tears. That was twelve years ago. So much time had passed. She was so good at pretending to be someone she wasn't. Did she even know how to be herself anymore? All that pretence had worked well for her over the years, but she wasn't that naive little girl anymore. Things had to change. She unconsciously ran her finger up the inside of her arm, tracing the thin silver scar which ran down the inside of her forearm. It was now almost invisible to the naked eye but she knew it was there. A constant reminder to her that Gary held all the power and wouldn't be happy to know she was leaving.

Gary set a pile of folded notes down on the edge of the table and nodded to her. She walked over and slid them off the table into her handbag. With a false smile she leaned over and kissed the top of his head.

"Thanks babe," she said, turning to go.

He grabbed hold of her wrist "You're not leaving are you?"

Her body tensed. The thought of having to have sex with him now repulsed her.

"I have an appointment."

His brow creased, "Well, later then?"

"Sure." She replied, knowing Gary wouldn't take no for an answer. He released her wrist. She gave Katrina and Rosie a wave. She would love to have told them she was leaving, but she couldn't risk Gary finding out.

"Take care you two." A lump caught in her throat. "Goodbye."

Katrina looked up, "See you. Maybe we can catch up tomorrow."

"That would be great. I'll ring you."

She glanced back at Gary, her brow creased. It was hard to

believe that she had once thought herself in love with him. It had been a time in her life when she had been too young and naive to know any better. In a way she guessed she would miss him. He had been there for her when she had needed it. If she had stayed on the streets, who knows what might have befallen her? She left the apartment thinking that maybe she was destined to be alone forever. Life as she knew it was about to change. That thought alone caused her to shudder. What did her future hold? She shook her head. It was best if she didn't think about it.

Gary sat at the desk counting his money, oblivious to the fact that his income was about to take a substantial hit. Carley had been a major part of his success. He grinned to himself, looking forward to her return. Over the years he had become obsessed with her and having her in his bed was one of the perks of being the one who paid the bills.

Carley hesitated at the top of the stairs. She glanced back at the closed door, doubt beginning to set in. Why was she doing this? Her past had helped mould her into who she was. Going back wasn't going to change that. As much as she wanted her life to change she wasn't sure she was ready. There would be no more hiding from the past and that thought alone terrified her beyond words.

Chapter Three

Carley turned towards her apartment. She needed to get out of the city and fast. Within the hour she had packed, showered and was standing in the open doorway. Her fingers tightened around the doorknob as she turned back to take one last look at her apartment. With a small sigh she pulled the door closed behind her. The keys to the red Porsche Gary had bought her for her birthday lay on the kitchen counter. There wasn't time to pack completely. Apart from the small suitcase she carried, all her possessions were now his. She hoped that that alone would be enough of an incentive for him not to follow her.

When she reached the street the taxi she had ordered was already waiting at the curb. As she approached the driver got out and walked around to the back of the cab. He smiled as he took her luggage and placed it in the trunk then opened the rear door for her.

"Thank you."

He nodded, "My pleasure madam."

She slipped into the seat. He closed the door behind her. Her phone chirped, she slipped it out of her pocket, and opened it. Her body tensed. It was Gary wanting to know what time she would be back. The taxi driver moved around to the driver's door and got in. He pulled away from the curb, entering the downtown traffic effortlessly. Carley glanced down at her phone, then opened the window and tossed it out onto the street. She looked back just in time to see it being run over by a car in the next lane. A smile creased her lips. She dropped her head back against the seat and closed her eyes. The taxi driver took the opportunity to study his passenger through the rear view mirror. Her brow creased, "I'd appreciate it if you'd keep your eyes on the road," she said, without even opening her eyes.

The taxi driver quickly averted his eyes, a puzzled expression crossing his face as he focused his attention back on the road.

Ten minutes later they were pulling into the bus station. Carley opened her eyes as the taxi drew to a stop. It felt a little ironic that as a young girl she had left home on a bus and was now returning on one. The driver got out and retrieved her luggage from the trunk placing it on the curb. She paid him.

"Thank you." She said giving him a warm smile.

Picking up her suitcase she hurried inside to collect her ticket. When she exited the building the bus was already waiting at the curb, so she hurried over. The young man loading the luggage looked up at her. His cheeks instantly coloured. Carley smiled reassuringly as she handed over her case to him. Avoiding her gaze he took it from her and loaded it into the compartment.

She entered the bus choosing a window seat near the back. The young man glanced up at her through the window. When she returned his gaze he quickly looked away. He probably wasn't much older than she had been when she had stepped off the bus into this big unforgiving city. It now seemed a life time ago that that frightened young girl had battled for her life on these dark and dangerous streets. It was a miracle that she had survived! Thinking about it only made her more determined to put her life back on track. She wasn't going to let her past dictate her future any longer. The bus pulled out of the depot. Her eyes turned to the window as they travelled through the city. A lump caught in her throat as she watched the last familiar landmark drift out of sight. Her head dropped back against the seat. She had finally done it.

It wasn't until she felt herself being gently nudged awake that she realised she had slept most of the way. Her eyes blinked open. The driver was standing above her.

He smiled "I think this might be your stop."

"Ooh... right, thanks," she replied, stretching her stiff limbs. Her top crept up giving him a glimpse of her flat tanned abdomen. She tugged it down, fully aware of what she saw in his bold stare. Her eyes narrowed as she got to her feet.

"After you," she said stiffly, motioning to the front of the bus.

He gave a small grunt then turned and headed out. When she got to the curb he had already tossed her case onto the pavement.

"Thanks for waking me."

"Sure," he grunted as he entered the bus.

She stood watching as the bus pulled away from the curb and disappeared over the rise. A cold shiver ran up her spine. With a deep sigh she slung her handbag over her shoulder and bent to pick up her suitcase. With a growing reluctance she headed off in the direction of her parents' house. A large sign stood at the beginning of the main street welcoming anyone who passed. She gave a strained little laugh. It would be a cold day in hell when she felt welcome here. Georgetown didn't hold any fond memories for her. Who in their right mind would want to live in a town where everybody knows everybody else's business?

An old red Ford pickup rattled past blasting its horn, making her jump. Her handbag slipped off her shoulder and the contents spilled out onto the ground. The truck barrelled away, flicking up a cloud of dust. A loud wolf whistle shrilled out through the driver's window. She shook her head, "Typical... welcome home Carley" she muttered to herself, as she bent to retrieve the spilt contents of her bag. "Welcome home."

Chapter Four

As she walked the along the path toward what used to be her family home, the memories began to flood back. After twelve years away, she was surprised to find that everything still felt very familiar. She had walked these streets on a daily basis. That same feeling of hopelessness that she had felt as a child was still there. Her eyes focused on the old neglected bungalow that stood nestled against a backdrop of thick trees. Didn't anything ever change in this backward little town? Even the huge two-storied colonial house that took pride of place about midway down the street looked exactly as it always had, right down its bright blue shutters and perfectly manicured lawns. She glanced at the empty overgrown lot next to it. The old ramshackle barn had gone. She remembered the night the house had burnt to the ground. For years afterwards the barn had stood alone, obscured by the dense bush surrounding it. Some of the neighbourhood children had been convinced that it was haunted, which had worked in her favour. Her eyes glistened. Many a tear had been spilt there, firstly for the loss of her mother but most of all for the little girl whose innocence had been stolen from her.

She shifted her suitcase to the other hand, as its weight began to bite painfully into the soft flesh of her palm. Her pace slowed as the street sign came into view. Did she really want to do this? The tension began to mount as she forced herself forward. She drew to a stop at the street corner. Her mouth went dry as she spied the letterbox further down the street. An icy chill settled over her. Many a time she had walked this path alone. With a growing reluctance she began to make her way down the street. After her mother's death the house had stopped feeling like home. The life had simply drained out of it. The kitchen had stood idle, and the rooms had been filled with faint memories of a time in her life when she had felt loved. She glanced across at a neighbouring house, sensing that she was being watched, or was it just her imagination playing tricks on her?

Dropping her suitcase at the gate, she stood staring up in disbelief. She checked the number on the letterbox. It was hard to believe it was the same house. It looked as if it had been abandoned for years, instead of weeks. Her mind drifted back. Had she not noticed its slow decline? Visions of an overgrown lawn and disappearing gardens entered her mind. Her chest tightened. Her mother would have hated to see it like this, she had always been house proud. Her eyes moistened as she took in the cracked and peeling paint. Some of the windows were broken and had been crudely covered by wooden boards. The lawns were almost knee high, and the weeds now towered well above the tips of the grass. Her fists clenched as she spied the remnants of her mother's garden, now almost completely lost under a thick covering of weeds. The windows of the house stared back at her like black soulless eyes. A cold shiver ran up her spine. "They're just windows" she muttered quietly to herself. Perspiration began to bead on her upper lip. Looking at the state the house was in she wondered why she had bothered. There was nothing for her here, except more pain and heart ache. She reached down and grasped the handle of her suitcase but found her body reluctant to move. "He can't hurt you anymore'" she mumbled, over and over again, as she took one tentative step after another. Grasping the hand rail she willed herself forward. After what felt like an eternity, she found herself standing at the front door; the last barrier between her and the past. Her suitcase dropped to the ground as she took in the depressing state of the door. Large cracks slashed their way across its once smoothly painted surface. Even the big brass door knocker which had always taken pride of place in the centre of the door now hung precariously by a single rusty screw.

A feeling of dread tugged at her remaining courage and she wanted nothing more than to run from this place and never look back. Tears welled in her eyes as she reached out and tried the door handle. A little hysterical laugh escaped her lips. It was locked. Instinctively she reached up to slide her hand along the top edge of the door frame. Her hand stilled when it met with the cold familiar shape of a key. Her heart began to pound in her chest. After all these years it was still right where she had left it. Lowering her hand, she stood motionless staring down at the key resting in the palm of her hand. With a sudden jolt she was transported back to her childhood. Her mother had only just passed away. It had torn at her heart to see the other children with their parents. They would come in droves to meet their children after school just as her mother had always done for her. The ones whose parents didn't come would walk off in groups, laughing and chatting as they went. Carley had struck a lonely figure walking home alone. Nobody seemed to care that she was hurting, lost in her own grief. Tears would trickle down her cheeks as she reluctantly trudged home to an empty house.

Her friends had slowly drifted away, unsure of what to say or how to be with her anymore. As the days passed she slowly withdrew from the outside world. Alone and frightened she struggled to live with the cold reality of death. Her father had been too lost in his own grief to notice his daughter's anguish, as he himself turned to alcohol to help dull his pain. Ignoring the needs of the little girl he had once loved so dearly.

She turned the key repeatedly in her hand then stepped towards the door and slipped it into the lock. The door gave a brief tortured groan as it opened, giving her a small glimpse of its dark uninviting interior. Drawing in a deep calming breath, she placed her palm against the door and gave it a good hard shove. A cold shiver ran up her spine as the black void opened up before her. The darkness loomed out at her and instinctively she stepped backwards. Would the demons from her past be waiting to devour what little courage she had left? She stood motionless, her eyes straining into the darkness, her breathing now coming in fast shallow gasps. A deathly silence filled the air. She jumped when a dog barked from somewhere down the street. Minutes ticked by with only the sound of her own heartbeat echoing inside her head. Summoning up all her remaining courage, she forced herself to step across the threshold. Her heart began to hammer away in her chest as she moved further into the darkness. She reached out and flicked the light switch. The room remained in darkness. A hard knot formed deep in the pit of her stomach as she cautiously made her way along the hallway. It was hard to make out her surroundings as the only light entering the room was from the open doorway behind her. Her nose wrinkled as the putrid smell of mould and stale alcohol assaulted her nostrils, repulsive to her yet so familiar. She put her hand across her mouth swallowing back the urge to vomit as she was slowly drawn back into the past. Vivid images of her father staggering home drunk, then vomiting on the floor where he had fallen entered her mind. Her heart rate began to climb as the darkness closed in around her. It was obvious to her now that she should not have come here. Her fists clenched as the all too familiar signs of panic began to take hold. The house reeked of him. Her heart drummed wildly in her chest. She gasped, imagining his hands reaching out of the darkness to grab at her. All her previous courage suddenly dissolved as she spun around to face the front door. The light streamed through the opening. She focused on the golden shaft of light and after a few long agonizing minute's her breathing began to ease. She glanced over at the covered windows. Taking a couple of tentative steps sideways whilst keeping her eyes firmly fixed on the open doorway, she slowly made her way toward them. As she shuffled her way across the room, small clouds of dust rose up and danced around her feet only to resettle on the floor once she had passed. When she could no longer see the front door she spun around and quickly made her way through the dimly lit room. Her throat tightened as the panic again began to set in. When she reached the covered windows she grabbed hold of the curtain and dragged it open. A small sliver of light stretched across the floor. Reaching for the next one she gave it a violent tug, letting out a startled gasp as it came away in her hand and fell into a heap at her feet. Clouds of dust flew up into the air and floated in the light now struggling through the filthy window panes. Her hand flew to her mouth as she took in the disgusting state of the room. Old food containers and bottles littered the floor. Cigarette butts trailed across the floor from empty overturned beer bottles. Thick layers of dust covered everything. Surprisingly though, the room looked very much as she remembered it. She nervously glanced towards the door, expecting that at any moment her father would stagger into the room and collapse in a drunken heap on the floor. Drawing her eyes from the door she slowly scanned the room. Avoiding the piles of rubbish littered across the floor, she made her way towards the sideboard. Curiously she picked up one of the photo frames and brushed her hand across the surface of the glass to remove the thick layer of dust that had accumulated there. Her hands tightened on the frame. It was a picture of her and her mother. It was her mother's smiling face that often haunted her dreams. Her sudden death was still a constant reminder of how quickly one's life can change.

Using the bottom of her shirt she carefully wiped the glass before placing it back down on the dresser. Her hands moved to the next frame. Again she used her shirt to wipe away the years of dust. It was an old class photo. Her eyes drifted along the rows of pupils. It had been taken the year after her mother had died. There was a sudden tightening of her chest as her eyes locked on one of the pupils. She remembered that smile. It all started to flood back. He had been her rock, her savour and the only person that had really given a damn about her. Her fingertips brushed across his image as she whispered his name. "Dean Baxter." It felt good to say his name after all these years. She had become so used to him being around that she had never really imagined what her life would be like without him. How had she ever found the courage to leave him? It hadn't taken her long to realise that leaving had been one of the biggest mistakes she had ever made; one that she would probably pay for for the rest of her life. After everything he had done for her she had simply turned her back on him and disappeared into the night. Her head shook slowly from side to side. She hadn't even had the decency to say goodbye.

The house and everything in it was like poison to her mind. For two years after her mother's death her father had been distant and uncaring, leaving her to face her grief alone. Then suddenly.... she shook her head, not wanting to think about what he had done to her. She had never had the courage to tell anyone about what had happened to her, right here in this house. Dean had been her closest friend and even he was oblivious to the hidden turmoil she faced after the lights went out. He had been the only good thing in her life and at the time she hadn't dared risk losing him. Her internal pain had remained deeply buried. Over time, she had learnt how to distance herself from reality, locking the real Carley behind a wall, where she knew she would be safe. A wall that to this day still sheltered her from the world.

Sobbing uncontrollably, she dropped the photo back down on the sideboard and turned for the door. Barely able to stand, she staggered out on to the front porch, slamming the door closed behind her. Her chest heaved as a fresh flood of tears spilled down her cheeks. Falling back against the door she clenched her fists and thumped them against it. Everything in this house reminded her of her father. If only she had had the strength to confide in someone back then. Now it was too late, the damage had already been done. Her father had used her love for him and turned it into something disgusting. A deep tremble vibrated through her body. When her mother was still alive, he'd do all the normal fatherly things. He would hug her and whisper "I love you" into her ear. The bedtime stories and the light kisses on the forehead as he tucked her into bed at night. He had taught her how to swim and ride a bike. This was how she wanted to remember her father. After her mother died, that had all changed. All the love and support she had grown to expect from her father had instantly ceased. Pushing herself away from the door, she snatched up her suitcase and headed out on to the street. She glanced back at the house. There was no way she could stay in there. A shiver ran up her spine. This time there was no mistaking it as she saw the curtains in the neighbouring house being suddenly drawn closed.

"That's right" she muttered to herself. "Where were you when the young girl next door was being abused by her father night after night?" She walked to the end of the road, turned left and headed toward the main street. Why was she even considering doing anything to the house? What was she hoping to achieve? Visions of the littered floor entered her mind. For months after her mother's death, she had survived on bread, peanut butter and water out of the tap. Occasionally her father would remember to shop for food. She would find herself hording it away, eating only what she had to, knowing before long the cupboards would again be bare. It had been a sad existence for a once happy child who had had a home and two loving parents.

Chapter Five

With red rimmed eyes she made her way down the main street pulling her suitcase behind her. People stopped what they were doing to watch her pass, whispering between themselves. There was no mistaking the family resemblance. Drawing her shoulders back, she drew in a deep breath. No way was she was going to let them see how much she was hurting. Their blatant cold stares told her in no uncertain terms that they didn't want her here. What right did they have to judge her? This was her birth place and she had just as much right to be here as anybody else. As a child she had played in these streets, visited their stores and some their homes. Her back stiffened as a woman passed by giving her a cold hard stare.

She pulled the motel door open and entered the reception area. Two older women sat on chairs talking to a plump cheery looking woman, behind the counter. Carley smiled as she entered. The two older women turned and looked at her, then quickly got their feet and exited through the door she had just entered, whispering quietly between themselves.

"Hi honey; what can I do for you?" the woman behind the counter asked.

"Oh," said Carley, still staring after the two women who had just left. "I'd like a room please" she finally asked. "What was their problem?" The woman shrugged "Who knows? Look Hon. don't worry about them. They have too much time on their hands and spend far too much of it poking their noses in where they are not wanted."

Carley turned from the door. The woman gave her a warm welcoming smile, "Now lovey. How long were you intending to stay?"

Carley hesitated, not having given it a thought. It was going to take her a lot longer to get the house ready for sale than she had first anticipated. She cringed at the thought of having to do the cleaning herself. Pride was a funny thing. As much as she hated the house there was no way she was going to let anyone from town see it in that state.

"Could you make it three weeks? If I needed more time could I extend my stay at a later date?"

The woman smiled, "Sure, I can't see any problem with that. I'm Nancy by the way. Welcome to Highways End."

Carley smiled "Thank you. I'm Carley Tanner."

"Nice to meet you Carley. Now, it'll be a straight five hundred dollars for the first week. You can settle the rest when you vacate your room." Carley pulled out her credit card and handed it over. Nancy put the transaction through then handed the card back.

"Now let's get you settled. If you would like to follow me I will show you to your room." Nancy said, stepping out from behind the counter. "During your stay if you have any problems no matter how small just call the office and we will get it sorted right away."

Carley nodded, giving a yawn. The thought of a nice comfortable bed seemed rather inviting. She followed Nancy along the path and down a narrow alley to the other side of the building.

"Here we are" she said, opening the door to one of the ground floor units.

Carley followed her into the room.

"Here's the key. Fresh towels are supplied every day. Breakfast is available if you wish. The menu is in the folder on the table. I'll leave you to get settled and remember if there is anything you need you can come down to the office or simply punch 07 on the phone. I hope you have a pleasant stay." She smiled then left closing the door behind her. Carley watched through the window as she made her way across the parking lot. She glanced around the unit. A small dining table and four vinyl chairs stood in one corner. On the other side of the room two compact low backed sofas were set in an L shape, their backs pushed up against the walls. They both faced a large wall mounted flat screen television. Dropping her suitcase by the door she walked into the bedroom. It was small, with only just enough space for the double bed, two bedside cabinets and a chest of drawers. The wardrobe and bathroom door stood side by side on one wall. She peeked in at the bathroom and smiled, small but functional. The tension slowly began to ease out of her shoulders. Exhausted she plopped down on the edge of the bed. It was a little firm but it would do. She dropped back on the bed, and lay there for a while, staring up at the ceiling. Her eyelids slowly closed.

She woke to find herself still fully clothed, lying on top of the covers. Nightmares had plagued her throughout the night. Placing her fingers at her temples she gave them a soft massage but it did little to alleviate the constant throbbing. Swinging her legs off the bed she drew herself into a sitting position. Her stomach grumbled. Her body swayed as she pushed herself to her feet.

"Damn him," she cursed as she headed for the bathroom for a shower.

The sooner this was all over, the better. Having to pay for her father's funeral was like another slap in the face. What had he ever done for her except ruin her life?

Fifteen minutes later she stepped from the shower feeling slightly more refreshed. Snatching the towel from the rail she quickly dried herself, then dropped it on the floor. She walked through to the kitchen. Her suitcase stood beside the door. She picked it up and made her way back to the bedroom, tossing it onto the bed. The case was only half full. Most of her good clothes had been left behind. As far as she was concerned, they belonged to a woman who no longer existed. She gave a heavy sigh as she pulled out a short black denim skirt. Stepping into it, she drew it up her legs and fastened it. She pulled on a white sleeveless top, tugging it down over her body. It fitted snugly, drawing attention to her narrow waist and full bust. Lastly she wriggled into a pair of skimpy lace underwear. Her hands glided down over her skirt as she tried to smooth out the wrinkles. Not wanting to fuss she left her hair to fall softly about her shoulders. She pursued her lip's running lip gloss across them. After pulling on her black ankle boots, she took one last look in the mirror and headed for the door.

The bright glare of the sun blinded her as she opened the door and stepped out into the sunshine.
"Good morning, isn't it's a beautiful day?" Nancy called from the doorway of one of the other units.
Carley smiled and gave a small wave. She had never been one for small talk, especially not with women. Truthfully, she had never really had any girlfriends, not since her mother had died. Katrina and Rosie had been the closest things to friends she had had and even they didn't really know her.

Carley had hoped to avoid having to go anywhere near the

funeral home but alas, they had phoned to say they needed to see her. He had mentioned something about final instructions. As she turned into the main street, her stomach grumbled. A quaint little cafe across the street caught her eye. She crossed the road and found herself hesitating at the door. Silence fell across the room as she entered. Pulling back her shoulders, she approached the counter.

The woman behind the counter smiled, "How can I help you?"

Carley could feel every pair of eyes on her, "A flat white and a ham and cheese croissant, thank you."

"Is that to have here or to go?"

Carley glanced about her, "To go."

"That will be five dollars, thank you."

Carley handed over the money, then snatched the bag from the counter and hurried out the door. Spotting the local park, she made her way over and finding the nearest seat slumped down onto it. She drew in a deep breath; her heart rate began to settle. What was it with this town? Why did they dislike her so much? She opened the bag. It felt good to get some food inside her, especially since she had not eaten since the previous morning. When she had finished she tossed her rubbish into a nearby bin and headed across the park. The sooner she could get out of this town the better for everyone, herself included. She gave a cynical little laugh at having to foot the bill for her father's funeral. He could have been buried in a pine box in the backyard for all she cared. If she didn't have to organize the house and its sale she would have handled the whole thing from the city. She gave a heavy sigh. At the very least she had to try and show some respect. It certainly wouldn't pay to alienate the whole town; at least, not before she had a chance to sell the house anyway. After all, this had been his home, and some of these people had known him most of his life. She gave a snort. Well, at least they thought they did. It looked as if a large proportion of the town already hated her for reasons she was still unsure of. So the less she did to aggravate the situation the better for everyone.

Chapter Six

It only took her a few minutes to get to the funeral home. She shoved the glass doors open and entered. A frail old man, stood at the counter, his back bent in a pronounced stoop. He looked up as the bell on the door jingled, and smiled, displaying a mouthful of missing teeth. He reached down under the counter and pulled out a set of false teeth, which he quickly inserted into his mouth.

"Sorry about that, I find them rather uncomfortable," he said smiling apologetically.

Carley wasn't quite sure what to say. The old man shuffled out from behind the counter.

"You must be Carley? If you don't mind me saying, you are the splitting image of your mother."

She nodded in acknowledgement, giving him a forced smile. With a wave of his little skinny arm, he gestured towards the back room.

"Why don't we go on through to the office so we can discuss the last few details of your father's funeral?"

Again she simply nodded, following him into the back room. Her eyes scanned the small and extremely cluttered room. A huge desk took up most of the space. Stacks of books had been arranged neatly around three side of the room, with not one book shelf in sight.

"Take a seat" he said pointing to a chair that had been carefully placed in the only free corner in the room. Stepping over a box of files she sat down and crossed one leg over the other.

"Well um...." the little man murmured. "We already have the service sorted and the burial plot has been prepared. There is just the final payment to organise. Oh... and there is also the matter of the eulogy. Was there anything you would like to say?" As he waited for her to answer, his eyes continually flicked from her face to her legs.

Her eyes narrowed, "Well, in that case we are finished. There is nothing I want to say, so if we can wrap this up I'll be on my way. The funeral's at ten o'clock is it not?"

He looked across at her. "Um yes, ten o'clock, that's right. Are you sure there is nothing you want us to say... on your behalf."

There were a few things she would like to say. However, she didn't think they would be appropriate for his funeral. "No! I have nothing to say. If you want to say something, by all means feel free to do so," she spat angrily.

He rose to his feet, "Right... Okay then. Shall we go through and sort out the payment, and then you can go and see your father." Carley froze, "What?" she snapped.

"Oh umm... I just assumed... that you would want see him... before the funeral," he stammered, feeling a little uncomfortable at her obvious annoyance.

"Well! You assumed wrong" she replied her voice rising to a feverish pitch "I don't want to see him. Is that clear enough for you?" The little man seemed at a loss for words as he quickly scuttled from the room. She followed after him and found him at the front counter shuffling papers around nervously.

Her brow creased. "Look I'm sorry; I didn't mean to yell at you." He stopped what he was doing and looked up at her.

"It's quite alright, I understand. Under the circumstances I would probably feel the same. I can see why this might be a little upsetting for you."

A frown creased her brow, "Circumstances? What circumstances?" She was starting to get rather irritated with the silly man.

He began to shuffle papers again.

"I asked you a question."

He stopped what he was doing and looked up at through his glasses that were now perched precariously on the end of his crooked little nose. Still he chose not to answer.

Her anger began to rise, "Well?" she hissed.

"I....I... I thought..Y.. your father..."

She gritted her teeth, "My father what?

"He... he... committed suicide."

Her eyes widened, "He what?"

The old man pushed his glasses up his nose nervously "He hanged himself... at h...home, I believe." Carley's body tensed. "People around here say it was from a broken heart."

Carley stared at him speechless.

He continued, "You know because of your mother being killed. Th...then... you just disappearing like that."

She stared at him, not knowing how to respond still unable to absorb what she had just heard.

He slid the bill cautiously across the desk. She glanced down at it. She opened her handbag pulled out her credit card and handed it over the counter to him. He put the transaction through, and she signed for it. Snatching her card back off the counter she turned to leave.

"If you're lucky, you might see me at ten."

A deep throaty laugh erupted from her lips as she exited the building. The old man stood staring after her, his mouth agape in disbelief. If it wasn't so laughable she would be angry, "Some people are so stupid", she muttered under her breath. "Died of a broken heart, now there's one for the books." If only they knew she thought to herself, if only they knew. She slung her handbag over her shoulder. Let them think what the hell they liked. She wasn't here to make friends. All she wanted was to get the damn house sold, so she could leave this stupid narrow minded little town. Let them continue to live their lives in ignorance. Why should she care what they thought?

When she arrived at the supermarket, she was in no mood for niceties as she stormed through the doors. Grabbing a shopping cart she began to make her way quickly through the aisles, grabbing items from the shelves. People had already noticed the strong resemblance to the woman most of them had known years ago, but not one of them made an effort to speak to her. Some even stepped to one side as she passed. For her, that was nothing new. After her mother had died, very few people had even bothered to speak to the tortured little girl who just needed a friend.

"Stuff the lot of them" she thought to herself. She didn't need them. She didn't need anybody. After going through the checkout, she grabbed the shopping bags off the counter and stomped off through the doors. Her mind was still reeling over what the funeral director had told her about her father. How dare he take the easy way out and leave her to deal with the fallout?

She ran up the front steps to the house and quickly unlocked the door. Throwing it open, she let it crash back against the wall. She strode into the kitchen with none of her previous caution and tossed the shopping bags down on the counter top. Striding over to the windows she yanked on the cord. The blinds lifted and light filled the room. Her heart sank as she glanced around her. It was hard to know where to start. Emptying the contents of the bag on the counter, she grabbed the packet of rubber gloves, tore open the packaging and pulled them out, snapping them over her hands. She stood in the centre of the kitchen and turned full circle. The room was in such a disgusting state it was hard to know where to start. When she walked over to the sink she nearly lost her breakfast. It was piled high with dirty dishes. Black furry mould covered the surface of every plate. The water which had collected in the bottom of the sink resembled thick pea soup and the stench was almost unbearable. How dare he let her mother's kitchen get into such a state? Anger bubbled inside her as she went in search of the big plastic washing pail her mum had used to take the clothes out to the washing line. Returning to the kitchen, she dumped all the dishes into it to be thrown out later. For three solid hours she worked like a maniac, scrubbing every surface until it shone, determined to get the kitchen to resemble the way her mother used to keep it. One rubbish bag after another was filled until finally she was finished. The kitchen gleamed. She turned to look at the pile of bulging rubbish bags at the door. There were going to be a lot more of those by the time she had finished. With a satisfied smile she sat down at the kitchen table. The room was now how she remembered it. Tears welled up in her eyes.... the only thing that was missing was the smell of her mother's home baking. She could remember sitting at this very table eating her breakfast. Her body stiffened. Her father would walk into the room and say "What's up kiddo" and ruffle her hair. She shuddered, not wanting to remember any of those ridiculous childhood memories. It just made what he had done to her even harder to accept. Erasing her father from her life was going to be a lot more difficult than she had first thought. Her eyes moved around the room. So she had cleaned one room, but she still had a houseful of painful memories to go. A shiver ran up her spine as she glanced over at the stairs. Going up there was going to be challenging. It had been like a prison for her with no means of escape. She got to her feet with a renewed determination. He was gone from her life for good. He couldn't hurt her anymore. Picking up the roll of rubbish bags she made her way into the next room. If she could just rid the house of him it would be as though he had never existed. She frantically began filling the bags. As each one was filled, it felt as though part of him had disappeared forever.

By the time she had finished the bottom floor, her body was soaked with sweat. Lifting the hem of her top she wiped it across her face. There wasn't much left. Anything that had even remotely reminded her of him had been disposed of. As for the furniture, it could all be donated to some worthy cause. She moved to the bottom of the stairs. Her breath caught in her throat. Gripping the banister tightly she began to climb, dragging the half filled rubbish bag behind her. With each step it became harder for her to push the past from her mind. "He can't hurt you anymore" she mumbled to herself as she climbed one step after another. When she reached the landing she stopped and drew in a deep breath. "You can do this" she said, trying hard to convince herself. Standing in the hall outside her parents' bedroom, she now wasn't sure she could. Reaching up she gave the door a gentle shove. It slowly creaked open. A horrified gasp escaped her, as the putrid smell of sweat, mould and stale alcohol assaulted her. Her hand flew to her mouth and she very nearly pulled the door closed again. But she wouldn't let him win, not this time. She stepped through the door. The room certainly wasn't going to clean itself. Slowly, the rubbish bag began to fill. Once she had finished her parents' bedroom, she moved on to hers. A cold shiver ran up her spine as she stripped the bed. She tried hard not to think about what had befallen her in the room. As she yanked off the bedding it tore in her hands. By the look of it they had been there since the day she had left. Turning in a slow circle she took in the objects in her room. There had been a time in her life when she had loved this room. Now she couldn't wait to get out of it. All that it had bought her was shame.

By the time she had finished, she had a pile of rubbish bags stacked at the back door. A heavy sigh escaped her lips. Originally she had thought about putting them at the front gate for collection, but looking at the pile, she knew that would now be impossible. Without a car she couldn't dispose of it herself. She smiled at the thought of the rubbish bags stuffed into her little red Porsche. She drummed her fingers on the banister rail. Her eyes turned to the back door. Pulling the door open she stepped out onto the back porch. The backyard was very overgrown and well hidden from prying eyes. Going back inside she began to drag the bags out, stacking them against the back of the house.

Chapter Seven

She dropped four of the bags into the centre of the yard and upended them, spilling their contents onto the grass. A decent sized mound formed consisting of clothing, sheets and paper rubbish collected from throughout the house. Screwing pieces of newspaper up into balls she stuffed them amongst the rubbish. With a satisfied smile she slipped the matchbox from her pocket. Pulling out a matchstick she struck it, cupping her hand around the flame as she lowered it to the paper. The flame caught easily. Her eyes brightened as she watched it slowly spread to her father's things. There was no sadness in her eyes as she watched the fire slowly consume his belongings. Within minutes it was well ablaze. A satisfied smile creased her lips; after all this time she was finally ridding herself of the past. Dragging another bag over, she emptied it onto the fire, then another. Each time she felt more empowered, as if she was taking back her life somehow. She gave a grim little laugh. He wouldn't win, not this time. A giant wall of flame rose up and danced before her. There was no fear as she watched it quickly consume everything in its path. She stood captivated by its ability to eliminate the past. The empty bags lay scattered at her feet. A slight smile curved her lips. She had won. The memories were slowly fading.

The fire took on a life of its own. Her skin glowed pink. The air turned hot and thick. Unable to draw her eyes away she stood transfixed as the flames danced before her. Thick black smoke billowed up into the air, creating an enormous dark stain against the brilliant blue sky. She gave a series of loud coughs. The smoke had now begun to fight its way down into her lungs. At a time when she should have felt fear she was surprisingly calm. All the painful memories were slowly fading. Her eyes closed as the smoke blanketed her. A sudden gasp for air only drew in more smoke. Her mind slowly drifted. It would be so easy to let it all end right here, right now. To finally be free. The intense dry heat began to irritate the back of her throat and her lungs were now struggling to function. There was no guiding light. No waiting lost loved ones, just a cold blackness closing in around her. Her eyes widened as she drew in a deep breath filling her lungs with smoke. Her knees buckled and she dropped to the ground. Gasping for air she tried to crawl to safety, but in the dense smoke she couldn't seem to get her bearings. The blackness slowly began to draw her in. Was this how her life would end. She tried to move but her limbs wouldn't respond. Had she left it too late? Was she was more like her father than she cared to admit?

Two strong hands grabbed her under the arms and she felt herself being drawn out from under the blanket of thick smoke. She gulped in a mouthful of fresh air, choking violently. An oxygen mask was placed on her face and she was gently lowered back down onto the grass. Her eyes closed as relief washed over her. Her throat contracted painfully every time she took a breath but she didn't care. She was just relieved to feel the warmth of the sun on her face again. Her lungs filled with clean air. The back of her throat felt raw. It frightened her to think of how close she had come to ending her life. She could hear movement all around her. When she opened her eye's she saw a large bulky figure silhouetted above her.

"How are you feeling?" asked a deep masculine voice.

She blinked, trying hard to focus against the blinding sun. He bent down and removed the mask. "I... am, f...ine," she managed to croak.

"You know you are very lucky to be alive" he said gruffly. She tried to sit up but her vision blurred and she dropped back onto the grass. He reached down and took hold of her arm, gently easing her into a sitting position.

"You need to take it easy. You inhaled quite a bit of smoke. A few more seconds and you would have been unconscious. And it's a sure bet that throat's feeling mighty tender right now. I really recommend you go to hospital and get checked out."

"I...m," she placed a hand to her throat, "f...ine."

He gave an exasperated sigh, "We'll see. And just so you know it's against my better judgement. You are from out of town I take it?" She nodded.

"Figures, you should know there's a fire ban on. It's a miracle you didn't take out the whole neighbourhood." He glanced over at the house, "But what I'd really like to know is what you're doing here. This house is empty, it belongs to..." His eyes widened as he turned back to her.

She gulped back the tears. It had been a very emotional day and she was fighting to show any semblance of control. The last thing she needed right now was a lecture from someone who had no idea what she had been through. With a bit of effort she struggled to her feet, swaying slightly. He reached out a hand to steady her.

Her eyes narrowed as turned to glare at him, shrugging him off. "I don't need your help. I'm sorry; I never intended for this to happen." She blinked trying to clear her vision. The sun moved behind a cloud. Her mouth dropped open as her eyes settled on his face. Her legs suddenly buckled from under her. He reached out and grabbed her around the waist, taking her weight against his body. He guided her over to the house and lowered her down onto the steps. Her heart was pounding in her chest. She could still feel his eyes on her. He reached down and took hold of her chin tipping her face up to his. His face softened. It had been a long time since he had looked upon that face. His breath caught in his throat, "Car...ley, is it really you?"

Her heart skipped a beat. Minutes passed as they stared at one another, neither of them willing to believe what was right in front of them. A frown crept across her brow. His intense gaze began to unnerve her. "Carley..., when did you get here?"

Her chest tightened. Why had she not even considered the possibility that he might still be here? He would have questions, ones that she had no intention of answering. He reached out to steady her as she rose to her feet. Again, she shook him off. He stepped back, unsure of what to do next.

"Of course it's me," she snapped, as she slowly backed towards the door. Her hand closed over the doorknob. She turned it and pushed the door open. Stepping inside she slammed it closed flicking the lock. The pounding of her heart vibrated against her chest. Steadying herself against the wall, she drew a deep calming breath and slipped to the floor. She drew her knees up to her chest and wrapped her arms around them.

Dean stood staring at the closed door unable to comprehend what had just happened. After all this time, nothing had changed, she was still running away from him. He reluctantly turned his attention back to his team. The old feelings that he thought he had put to rest had come flooding back the instant he looked into her eyes. His brow creased. What did it all mean? Was he simply reacting to past emotions or was it possible..., he glanced back at the door; that after all this time he was still in love with her? He shook his head trying to clear his thoughts. Many hours had been spent thinking about her and fearing for her safety. Twelve years was too long to have to wait for anybody. Why had she not contacted him on her return? One of the men walked over to him. He glanced over at the house.

"What's her problem? She didn't seem very grateful."

Dean shrugged his shoulders "Who knows? I'll check on her before we leave."

"Do you know her?"

"We went to school together."

The man clapped his hand on Dean's shoulder, "It was a long time ago... people change."

Dean looked back at the house "And some don't." He turned his attention back to the damage the fire had caused. The garden shed hadn't faired very well, but otherwise no real damage had been done. At least they had managed to rescue the tools which he stowed safely under the house. She had been very lucky. If they hadn't come along when they had, it would have been too late to save her. His body stiffened. What if she had intended to kill herself? He pushed the thought aside, hoping he was wrong.

Even with her hair all tangled, eyes red rimmed and dirt smeared across her face there was no mistaking her beauty. He still regretted making the silly clumsy advances he had, as a young boy and often wished he could have taken it all back. When he realised he had fallen in love her it had taken him completely by surprise. A frown creased his brow. If only he had had the sense to tell her, instead of frightening her like he had. Maybe then things would have turned out a little differently. When her father had told him she had gone, he hadn't been ready to believe it. He was so sure that she would never have left without at least saying goodbye. For two long years he had waited for her to return. He would spend hours alone down by the lake drawing what little comfort he could from the time they had spent together. As the months slowly passed he began to accept the fact that she wasn't coming back. He had tried to move on with his life and convince himself that he didn't care, but in reality Carley had been one chapter in his life that he had been unable to close. Slipping off his jacket he walked over to the tap. Leaning forward he let the cool water run over the back of his head and down his neck. He had questions he needed answers to, but seeing her reaction to him today he wasn't sure if he would ever get them.

Carley heard the movement outside the window. Rising to her feet she peered out through the net curtain. A little involuntary gasp escaped her lips. He was standing only a few feet away, with only a pane of glass between them. The guilt hung heavily upon her. How easily she had tossed him aside. She braced herself against the window frame. He was real and no longer just a memory. When she had looked into those eyes all the years had simply fallen away. Tears welled in her own eyes. She had always felt so safe and protected around him. Her body stiffened, and so.... loved. Her hand went to her mouth. He had loved her..., and she him even if she hadn't realized it at the time. Her body began to tremble. How had she ever managed to leave him? She stepped up to the window. He certainly wasn't a young boy anymore. A quiver ran through her body as she took in his strong square jaw and full lips. His shoulders were broad and his chest wide. The pronounced muscle in his arm flexed as he ran his hand through his wet hair. Her teeth clamped down onto her bottom lip. The lanky young boy was now just a memory replaced by a man who was so close to perfection it was almost unbelievable. His deeply tanned skin glistened in the sunlight. Her hand gripped the edge of the curtain. Unwilling to torment herself any longer she reluctantly turned away.

A loud impatient knock sounded at the front door. A quick glance out the window told her who was on the other side. Swiping away her tears, she quickly made her way towards the door. Her heart rate increased. Cautiously she opened the door. White knuckled she gripped the doorknob. He smiled, causing her cheeks to flush. He reached up and brushed aside a wet lock of his hair, causing a small quiver to run up her spine. Thankfully he had slipped his jacket back on. Her brow creased, but he hadn't bothered to refasten it. The white singlet he wore underneath was damp and clung invitingly against his beautifully contoured chest and abdomen. Her teeth clamped together. He cleared his throat. Tearing her eyes away, she glanced up at him. He raised one eyebrow mockingly. Two small creases appeared at the corners of his mouth as he tried to stifle a smile. Her face flushed. She had been gawping she realized, as she shifted uncomfortably under his gaze. How was it that he could stand there looking so calm and relaxed when she felt such a blithering idiot? Feeling a little overwhelmed she took a small step backwards.

"What do you want?" she said rather more abruptly than she had intended. Just being around him was throwing all her emotions into turmoil. Her brow creased; if he would just stop smiling at her that way. Why did he have to go and drop back into her life when she had so much else to deal with? His smile faded, but his eyes stayed locked on hers.

"I just wanted to check you were okay. You gave me quite a scare and you did inhale quite a bit of smoke. I still think it would be wise to get you checked out."

Her body relaxed a little, he sounded genuinely concerned. How could she fault him, after all the kindness and the support he had given her after her mother's death. She blinked back tears.

"Look... as you can see... I'm fine."

He stood staring at her. Unable to meet his gaze she looked past him onto the street.

"Was there anything else?" Her question was met with silence but still she couldn't bring herself to look at him.

His body tensed, he wanted nothing more than to pull her into his arms again just like he used to. He stiffened, well, maybe not exactly like he used to. He had only been an inexperienced young boy then. His heart clenched. It was obvious she didn't want anything to do with him. He had been hoping for something that obviously wasn't there. He pushed himself away from the wall, "Goodbye Carley, take care." She watched him make his way down the path wondering why it was that she couldn't even bring herself to thank him. No matter how hard it was for her, he didn't deserve this.

"Dean" she called as she hurried down the path after him. He turned back expectantly. Leaving a safe distance between them she drew to a stop. "Thank you." she said giving him a weak smile. He looked her straight in the eye and smiled "Anything for you Carley, you know that."

He took a step towards her. She drew in a sharp breath as his hand brushed lightly down her arm.

"You don't know how good it is to see you again."

A powerful jolt shot through her and she had to fight the urge to leap away from his touch. He smiled then turned and walked away. He climbed aboard the Fire Truck and closed the door behind him. Carley felt the heavy weight of guilt settle on her shoulders. How could he possibly still care about her? Everything would be so much easier if he hated her. At least, then she might be able to keep all her emotions where they belonged in the past.

By the time she finally got back to the hotel, the anger had returned. Why couldn't she stop thinking about him? It was obvious by her reaction today that she was going to have to keep her distance.

Seeing him again would only complicate matters. But would she be able to stay away, she wondered? She had always seen herself as an experienced woman who knew how to handle men. Seeing Dean today had certainly proved that theory wrong. What if he was married? He could even have kids. Her shoulders slumped. She didn't want to think about him with another woman and there certainly wasn't any point in dreaming about something that could never be. Giving a long sigh she headed for the bathroom. When she caught her reflection in the mirror she almost cried. Puffy red rimmed eyes stared back at her. The fact that her face was covered in dark smudges and her hair was sticking out at peculiar angles only helped to deflate her all the more. Pulling off her clothes she tossed them on the floor in the corner. She turned the shower on and stepped in.

Chapter Eight

Carley lay on her back staring up at the ceiling. It was still dark outside. She guessed it to be sometime in the early hours of the morning. Turning on her side she thumped at her pillow. In a few hours, she would be attending her father's funeral. A deep seated anger burned deep down inside her. How could he have taken his own life and left her here to deal with the fallout he had created in hers? He had taken the easy way out and to make things worse, most of the town's people seemed to think he had been a good decent man. For the best part of the night, she had tossed and turned, unable to get the thought of his funeral out of her mind. Having to face all those people and pretend she cared. Adding to that was the shock of seeing Dean again. Giving a long groan she lifted the pillow up and placed it over her head.

"Go away," she shouted into the pillow. Who was she kidding; wasn't her life already messy enough? If Dean had even the faintest idea of what lay buried deep inside her he would run for the hills. There was certainly no chance of her telling him. No, her best plan of action would be to stay as far away from him as possible.

Finally sometime in the early hours of the morning her eyes closed, only to fly open again an hour later to the shrill ringing of the alarm clock. She groaned. Tugging the pillow out from under her head she threw it at the bedside cabinet, knocking the clock to the floor. It rolled just out of reach and continued its high pitched shrill. Throwing off the covers she staggered over and retrieved it from the floor, slamming her hand down on the button. Setting it down on the bedside cabinet she slumped back down onto the edge of the bed. Dropping her head into her hands she let out a long groan. A constant pounding hammered against her temples. Reaching over she snatched her handbag off the floor and searched through it. With a relieved sigh she pulled out a strip of pain killers. She popped three in her mouth and almost immediately began gagging as her dry mouth made it impossible to swallow them. Leaping off the bed, she staggered into the bathroom and turned on the tap, sucking in a large mouthful of water as she downed the tablets. Bracing herself on the edge of the sink she closed her eyes and let her head drop forward. The room stopped spinning and the dizziness eased. A quick glance in the mirror confirmed that she looked as bad as she felt. She headed back to the bedroom and sat down onto the edge of the bed. Damn him. Why now? Surprisingly, the clock was still reliably ticking away beside her. There was still time to make herself at the very least mildly presentable. She gave a little cynical laugh. People would think she was deep in grief, when to be honest she was far from it. The pain killers were beginning to kick in, except now her stomach felt a little queasy. Maybe it would have been a better idea to have eaten something before downing three tablets.

"Oh, today is going to be so much fun" she said sarcastically as she headed to the kitchen to make a coffee. Her mind turned to the coming funeral. It had been a huge mistake to come back here. She didn't owe her father anything. His funeral was simply a formality that she could have arranged over the phone. Dropping her mug into the sink, she headed back to the bedroom. She certainly didn't owe him any respect. He certainly hadn't showed her any. Maybe it had been simple morbid curiosity that had made her come back home? Or maybe it was because she had to see for herself that he was gone from her life for good.

Staring at her image in the mirror only bought back painful memories of the mother she had lost. Her face held the same soft facial features adorned with identical blue almond shaped eyes. Even her hair fell in soft dark curls around her shoulders just like her mother's had. Her body tensed as a car horn sounded out side. She walked to the front window and drew back the curtain. The taxi was waiting at the end of the drive. Her eyes flicked to the clock. Twenty minutes. That should be just about do it. There was no way she was going to arrive early and have to stand there and be ogled by everyone. Opening the door she stepped outside. As she went to pull it closed, she remembered her sunglasses and shot back inside to get them. The walk to the taxi seemed endless. She strode with a purposeful stride, trying hard to appear calm when she felt anything but. Her stomach clenched as she reached the taxi. The driver stood with the door open allowing her to quickly slide into the seat. A small sigh of relief escaped her as he closed the door behind her. It felt good to now be hidden behind the tinted glass where she couldn't be seen.

"All set?" the driver asked, returning to his seat and glancing up at her through his rear view mirror. He had watched her cross the car park, finding it impossible to draw his gaze from the long lines of her slender thighs that extended invitingly beyond the short hemline of her tight black skirt. Carley's eyes narrowed as they met his in the mirror. He smiled then quickly looked away. So many times she had been told she was beautiful, liars all of them. People say that beauty is in the eye of the beholder, but she had always believed that beauty came from within and on the inside she felt only ugliness. For years now she had hidden behind her good looks. Her whole existence was based on lies designed for one reason and one reason only; to cover up her past. She had been living a lie for so long now that her life often felt devoid of any semblance of truth. Over the years she had become dependent on her ability to close off her emotions, something she was finding harder to do, the longer she stayed in Georgetown.

"Cartwright Cemetery please, there's no rush" she snapped. The driver turned the vehicle around and headed back through town. There was no uniformity to the stores, which lined each side of an unusually wide street. They ranged from two storied buildings built in the early nineteen hundreds, to ones that resembled barns more than stores. Empty lots randomly appeared between the groups of stores for no apparent reason. She could still remember some of the stores from her childhood. It was obvious that life moved rather slowly around here, compared to the city. A few new businesses had sprung up in the town centre consisting of a small garage and towing company, a hair salon and the supermarket she had visited the day before. If it could be called that, it was no bigger than some of the small convenience stores in the city. A shiver ran up her spine, everything looked so familiar. The town she had known as a child hadn't really changed all that much. As they came up on the school she asked the driver to pull over to the side of the road. It too looked very much as she remembered it. A couple of extra classrooms had been added and the administration block looked as though it had a bit of work and part of the playground had been swallowed up by a tennis court. She blinked back tears as she recalled standing at these very gates waving to her mother. That had been the last time she had seen her. Feeling a sudden loneliness wash over her, she asked him to drive on. Her eyes watched the school gates disappear from view. Dwelling on the past certainly wasn't going to bring her mother back or change the hurt her father had caused.

Her body tensed as they drove in through the cemetery gates. The taxi driver pulled to a stop in front of the funeral parlour. A large group of people were already gathered at the front of the building. She took the time to scan the crowd. Her stomach tightened as she realised she didn't know any of them. A couple of faces looked vaguely familiar, but not enough for her to know who they were. The amount of people waiting had taken her by surprise. It was hard for her to accept that her father had actually had friends, people who obviously thought that he was a good person. If only they knew, she thought. Would they still be here? She slipped on her sunglasses, choosing to hide behind the safety of their dark tint. Eyes began slowly to turn in her direction. Her heart rate steadily began to climb. A small trickle of perspiration trickled down the back of her neck. Now that she was here, she wasn't sure if she could do it. Suddenly the door opened, giving her little choice. The driver stood patiently waiting. Every pair of eyes were now focused on her. Her hand shook as she reached for the door frame for support. Could they see her shame? She suddenly felt like a fraud. Did she even have the right to be here? Anger began to bubble deep down inside her. As much as she hated to admit it, she needed to do this; if not for her father, then for herself. Slowly she extended her legs out of the cab. If they felt the need to judge her, then let them. She knew the truth and that was all that mattered. It was her father who had helped make her into the woman she was today. He had taken her childhood dreams and her innocence and crushed them. Silence settled across the crowd as she got to her feet. The taxi driver closed the door, leaving her no means of escape. Out of the corner of her eye she saw the taxi move off. She dared a glance into the crowd. There were no friendly faces to give her the support she so desperately needed, but would never dare ask for. At this precise moment she didn't even know if there would be any other family members present. Her Aunty she hadn't seen since the day her mother had died, and she had no idea if there were any other living relatives. Drawing in a deep breath she squared her shoulders and took the first step to what seemed like the longest walk of her life. All eyes followed her movements as she made her way through the crowd. Her eyes didn't stray from the entrance. Faint whispers drifted in the air as she made her way towards the large wooden doors. People couldn't help but notice the striking resemblance to her late mother. She walked with a deliberate lengthy stride, her hips swaying seductively in her short tight black skirt. Her silk blouse was cut low in front giving a good glimpse of cleavage. Her tapered jacket hugged her waist accentuating the feminine curves of her frame. The five inch heels she wore only helped to draw attention to her long slender legs. She hesitated momentarily when she reached the door. A small sigh escaped her lips Ahead of her stood rows and rows of empty pews. Her eyes moved to the coffin resting on a raised platform at the front of the chapel. Drawing in a deep breath she slowly released it, "You can do this," she whispered quietly to herself.

The sound of her heels clicking on the wooden floor echoed around the room as she made her way up the centre aisle. She came to a stop beside the coffin. A large bouquet of flowers adorned the centre of the dark mahogany lid. They were only thing she had insisted on. She gently stroked a petal between her finger tips. The bouquet was beautiful, a mixture of lilies and carnations, two of her mother's favourites. Her fingers trailed over the gold inscription plate. "Gary Matthew Tanner" she said aloud to the empty room. Still she felt unable to shed a single tear for the man who used to call himself her father. Glancing up, she caught sight of his image staring back at her from the gold plated photo frame sitting on top of his coffin. She shivered. He appeared much older than she remembered. His hair had been almost completely grey and he seemed thinner, his skin more wrinkled. Dull lifeless eyes stared out at her. His mouth was set in a thin line making his whole face appear almost expressionless. He looked frail and old and held very little resemblance to the man she had once known. He had always been so big and strong and even frightening at times. She forced herself to look away. Why did she feel no sorrow? Had her heart finally turned to stone or was it that she was permanently scarred and incapable of love? Her father was dead and she didn't care. She turned away from the coffin and walked along the front isle. When she reached the middle, she sat down crossing one thigh over the other.

After a few minutes she became aware of the quiet whispers growing increasingly louder as people began to enter the room. The pews behind her slowly began to fill with his so called friends. She suddenly felt alienated. Where did she belong? Was there anywhere she could actually call home? Small doubts began to creep in as the whispers slowly grew louder. Her body gave a little shiver as little by little she felt the cold hatred building up behind her. All rationality began to leave her. She was now trapped in a room full of strangers. Her hands bunched into fists, drawing ever tighter with each passing minute. Tiny blood spots appeared at the tip of her nail as they dug into the palms of her hands. Closing her eyes, she tried to focus on the pain as the strong urge to run from the room tugged at her. Her body tensed; there was no escaping. She glanced across at the empty pew opposite, hoping beyond hope that at least one other family member would arrive to take this unbearable burden from her. The minutes slowly ticked by, but the pews remained empty. Reality hit her like a locomotive. She was going to have to face this all alone. A sob caught in her throat. Why was she putting herself through this? Why hadn't she simply stayed away until after the funeral?

All she could hear now was the constant thumping of her own heart. Tears threatened to spill over her lids. She blinked them back determined not to shed even one single tear for him. If any tears were to be shed it would be for the little girl that had endured more than a child should have had to, and survived. Her head began to pound as her headache returned with a vengeance. The room slowly begin to spin. Her hand flew to her mouth as she swallowed the urge to vomit. The whispers behind her grew even louder. She was now trapped, having to witness something she neither wanted to nor had the strength for.

A loud buzz rose throughout the room as a shadow fell across her knee. She glanced up and let out a startled gasp. Dean smiled down at her.

"I thought you might need some company," he said dropping down beside her.

Her mouth opened but no sound came out. He lent back and slid his arm along the top of the pew behind her, stretching his legs out in front of him. Her body tensed. Could she handle being so close to him along with everything else that had been thrown at her today? Her body began to shake uncontrollably. The music started and the minister entered the room. He nodded to her as he passed and headed up to take his place behind the pulpit. Dean dropped his hand on to her shoulder and gave it a reassuring little squeeze. He wrapped his other hand around her tightly clenched fists. She didn't have the strength to fight him. Her shoulders slumped. The minister began to speak. The shaking slowly began to subside. For the first time since she had stepped through that door she felt she might just be able to see it through. Her hand slowly relaxed she stretched her fingers out. His slipped his strong tanned fingers between hers. That simple gesture gave her the courage she needed. She glanced over at him. He was focused on the proceedings at the front of the room. All the sounds around her fell to a dull murmur as the years suddenly dropped away. Her eyes fell to where his hand was entwined in hers. As if reading her thoughts he turned to look at her, giving her hand a gentle squeeze. She tilted her face up and looked into those trusting eyes, as she had done so many times before. A sudden flicker of guilt shot through her. She hadn't wanted to think of how her disappearance might have affected him. He smiled at her, causing a small quiver to run up her spine. Luck had befallen her when he had so unexpectedly dropped into her life all those years ago. Her eyes glistened. Now, here he was again supporting her when she needed it the most. Her brow creased, but why? After everything she had put him through?

The rest of the ceremony became a blur. All she could think about was him and what she had lost all those years ago. She was only vaguely aware as some of the townspeople got up to say a few words about her father. A single tear trickled down her cheek but it wasn't for her father, it was for the young girl who never got to experience that first treasured kiss. That one precious moment which was now gone forever. Suddenly tears were streaming down her face. Dean handed her a pack of tissues. How was she ever going to move on from her past, when a big part of it was now sitting here right next to her?

The service ended. Carley gently wiped away her tears, taking a couple of deep breaths to try and calm her nerves. Dean stood, taking both her hands in his he drew her to her feet. She glanced up at him. He leaned down and whispered in her ear. "You can do this Carley. I know you can." He took her arm and guided her down the aisle. When they got to the door, they stood watching as the coffin was loaded into the hearse. A woman stood beside the door giving people directions to the burial site. Everyone began to move off towards their cars. Without asking, Dean led Carley across the car park to his pickup truck. He held her hand firmly as he opened the passenger's door and helped her inside. He had always looked out for her and had slipped back into that role with simple ease. She slumped in the seat; a cold numbness settling over her. The upheaval of last few days was beginning to take its toll.

The house, the funeral and now Dean, it was all becoming too much to process. Her eyes followed him as he walked around to the other side of the truck and slipped into the driver's seat. His brow creased. She looked so drawn and pale. He reached over and gently placed a reassuring hand on her knee just as he had done so many times before. She let out a startled gasp and snatched it away.

"I'm sorry." He said placing his hand back on the steering wheel, cursing silently to himself. She wasn't the same Carley he remembered, and the sooner he realised that the better. Her gaze turned to the window. Nothing had prepared her for the hot flash that had shot across the surface of her skin at his touch. Her hand settled down over her knee. That wasn't the reaction she had been expecting. A small sigh escaped her lips. She couldn't deal with this right now. Her head began to throb. Why had she reacted in that way? A deep groove appeared in her brow. Obviously her first suspicions had been correct. She couldn't trust herself to be around him. Over the years she had managed to convince herself that she was the one in control and all the choices were hers. In the last couple of days her life seemed more like endless moments of lost control and very little in the way of choice. She glanced across at him, unsure of what had just happened. His eyes met hers, her cheeks heated.

"I'm sorry, I shouldn't have done that."

Giving him a half hearted smile she turned away.

"There's no need to apologise. No harm done."

"It's taking a little getting used to, seeing you again it has been quite a shock to the system."

She nodded, "I know what you mean."

"If you're feeling up to it, I think maybe it's time we headed up to the grave site."

She gave him another weak smile. "I'm fine, honestly."

He smiled. "That's what you said last time I asked."

"Well, maybe you need to stop asking."

He started the truck and headed up the hill, while she sat quietly, staring out the side window. They slowly made their way up the steep road to the top of the cemetery. It was very unsettling for her to be sitting next to him in his truck. She glanced over at him, suddenly wishing more than anything that she had experienced that first treasured kiss with him. Now it was far too late to go back and collect it. So much had happened since they had last seen each other. They had both lived very different lives.

It appeared that everyone was waiting for them. Dean pulled his truck up behind the other cars. Carley made no effort to get out. He came around and opened her door, gently taking her by the hand. She glanced up at him, her eyes moist.

He squeezed her hand. "I'll be with you the whole time. It'll be okay." He led her across the grass to the freshly dug grave. Numbly she stood looking at the coffin, only mildly aware of the people standing behind her. All she could think about was how her hand fitted into his. Like two pieces of a puzzle. She noticed he didn't wear a wedding band. Her chest tightened. It was disturbing to think of him holding someone else's hand as he now held hers. Or making love to another woman. Her grip tightened on his hand.

He looked over at her pale face, "Be strong, it is nearly over."

Blinking back the tears she tried to concentrate on the proceedings. She had no claim on him no matter how much she wanted it.

Chapter Nine

As they lowered the coffin into the ground, tears began to trickle down her cheeks. Surprisingly they were for the father that had once loved her like a father should. She could remember him on the school sports days. He would stand on the side line cheering her on. Every Sunday he would take her down to the local park to play on the swings. All the things a daughter would expect from her father. She walked to the edge of the grave just as the coffin came to rest at the bottom. Slipping her hand from Dean's she bent to pick a flower out of the basket. Her eyes followed it as it dropped down onto the lid of the coffin. Tears continued to trickle down her cheeks.

"Goodbye Daddy" she whispered, then abruptly turned and headed back to the truck. Dean came up beside her and slipped his hand into hers, leaving the other mourners watching after them.

"You're not staying?"

She shook her head. He opened the door and helped her into the truck. Her eyes stared vacantly out the window, not knowing how she was supposed to feel? Should she be angry with him for taking her innocence, feel sadness for the loss of her father, or pity for what he had become? Part of her felt relieved that it was finally all over. She glanced back at the grave site with a heavy heart. Her family no longer existed. Dean got in beside her and turned the key in the ignition, "Everybody's heading back for something to eat and drink, do you feel up to it?" She shook her head slowly, "I just want to go back to the motel and forget this day ever happened."

He so much wanted to take her in his arms and comfort her, but he knew he couldn't. "Have you got a lift back to the motel?"

"What? Oh, no..., I was just going to call a taxi."

He frowned. "Don't be silly, I'll run you home."

She nodded. A puzzled expression crossed his face; something was wrong, he could feel it. It was more than just her father's death, she seemed lost and distant.

They pulled up in front of the motel and he cut the engine. In the silence that followed the tension slowly began to build. She placed her hand on the door handle.

"Well, thank you again. You always seem to turn up just at just the right moment" she paused for a second. "Come to think of it, you always did have an uncanny knack for turning up at the most opportune moments." Dean smiled, "It's all in the timing."

Her eyes turned to his, "It took me by surprise..., you still being here." He looked over at her, suddenly realising why it was he had stayed. "I like it here. I have a good job, a house and friends that I've known most of my life."

Her body tensed, he hadn't mentioned a wife or kids. As much as she wanted to ask she couldn't bring herself to do it.

Maybe it was because she really didn't want to know the answer. Her eyes again shifted to his left hand. No wedding band or any sign there had ever been one. Her heart gave an involuntary flutter, as a small sigh escaped her lips. She didn't want to think of him sharing his life with someone else. Her hand wrapped around the door handle, part of her wanting to stay. "It meant a lot having you there today. I don't know if I could have managed it without you."

He gave her a warm smile; "Anytime." He wished he could stop worrying about her, but it seemed so ingrained in him and she looked so sad and lonely. It took all his strength to stop himself reaching out to touch her. He had made that mistake once already today and he wasn't about to do it again. The one question he needed to ask burned inside him, but knew now wasn't the time. His fingers tightened on the steering wheel. Was the Carley he remembered now just a memory? She opened the door and slipped out of the truck. She needed him, he could see that but what about what he needed? He watched as she walked to her room. The gentle sway of her hips, her long slender legs, how could any man not want her? Her shoulders drooped, the weariness evident. She paused at the door and turned to give him a small wave before disappearing inside and closing the door behind her.

He thumped the steering wheel. He could see how much of a toll the day had taken on her. If he could take away all her hurt he would, without a second thought. With a quick turn of the key the truck roared to life. Reluctantly he turned towards home. A home he had always hoped to share with her. He knew now that he was still in love with her and probably always would be. His brow creased. She seemed only a shadow of the girl he had once known. His mind drifted back to their last time together. Had he been so wrapped up in his own raging hormones that he had failed to see that something was wrong? Had he unintentionally let her down? For years afterwards the scene had played over and over in his head as he had tried to come up with answers. Was it something he had done? His grip tightened on the wheel. That would at least explain why she had reacted the way she had when he had touched her. If she would just trust him enough to talk to him. He desperately wanted her back in his life, but he wasn't about to rush into anything. She had broken his heart once already and he wasn't about to let her do it again. Besides that, he didn't even know if she actually had any intention of staying.

She leant back against the door, tears streaming down her face. Dean had been so wonderful today. Any woman would be lucky to have him, any woman but her. She cursed under her breath knowing it could never be. As far as she was concerned she was damaged goods and he certainly deserved better. Tossing her handbag down on the couch she flicked off her shoes. She yanked the fridge open and took out five of the mini bottles of alcohol from the door. Opening the first one, she emptied the contents in one long gulp, choking as the burn slid down her throat. She threw herself down on the sofa and opened the second bottle, which she also emptied in much the same fashion as the first. Not the best way to take spirits, but she wanted the day to simply disappear. The alcohol was absorbed into her system quickly, soothing her jagged nerves and dulling the ache in her heart. Her life was a total mess. She opened the third, spilling a little as she did so. Tipping the bottle she let the liquid run down her throat, the tension slowly began to leave her body. She opened the fourth bottle, downing it. Now unchecked the anger returned. Flashbacks from her past flicked to life in front of her. She threw the empty bottle against the wall. It bounced off and rolled across the floor. The contents of fifth bottle went down the same way as the others. The room spun as she struggled to her feet and staggered across to the room. Pulling the door open she stumbled outside, slamming it closed behind her. She ran up the drive in a clumsy blind panic and out on to the street trying desperately to escape her demons. Tripping several times, she fell to her knees, but the pain didn't register. She gave little thought to where she was going until she stumbled through the gate. Tears trickled down her cheeks. "Mom," she whispered softly as she tripped up the steps and landed in an untidy heap on the front porch. Cursing loudly she reached out for the wall, and supported herself against it as she slowly rose to her feet. Her hands gripped the doorknob. She pulled frantically at it, crying out in frustration when she realised it was locked. Reaching up she ran her hand along the door frame. The key wasn't there. Clenching her fists she thumped them against the closed door. Her body fell against it in defeat.

"Mom," she cried. Her eyes turned to the boarded window. Pushing away from the door, she stumbled along the veranda. Taking hold of the corner of one board, she tugged as hard as she could. The board held fast. She let out a frustrated scream as she reached for it again and pulled harder. Staggering backwards she tossed the board over the railing onto the grass. Scrambling through the open frame, she landed with a heavy thud on the other side. An incoherent mumble escaped her lips as she struggled to her feet.

"Mom, Mom, where are you?" she called as she wove her way through the house, bumping into the furniture as she went. As she staggered through the bottom floor, tears began to roll down her cheeks. Periodically she would fall silent waiting for a reply, but was only met with the eerie silence of an empty neglected house. She climbed the stairs to the second floor and walked along the hall stopping outside her bedroom door. A cold shiver ran up her spine. She shoved the door open.

"Mommy," she whispered as she stepped across the threshold. The house remained silent. She slumped down on the edge of the bed, her bare feet resting on the cold varnished floorboards. It didn't register that the bloodied bruised feet she was looking at, were actually hers. Blood dripped on the floor from a nasty gash in her knee, but she felt no pain. The alcohol in her system was making it impossible for her to think rationally. The room began to close in around her. She glanced towards the door expecting to see her father's large figure fill the frame. Panicked she looked for a means of escape, already knowing there wasn't one. Her eyes moved to the small dresser beside her bed. Reaching over she slid open the top drawer and began to frantically search through its contents. She withdrew her hand. Tears filled her eyes as she looked down at her closed fist. One by one her fingers opened. She sat motionless staring down at the little beaded bracelet sitting in the palm of her hand. Dean had given it to her on her fourteenth birthday. It was only made of cheap plastic but at the time it had meant the world to her, and still did. She slipped it onto her wrist and held it up to the light. Her father had forgotten her Birthday yet again and she was missing her mother terribly. Dean had given it to her after school, along with a little cup cake with a candle in it. He had even embarrassed himself by singing Happy Birthday to her very badly. It had made her laugh. She swivelled the bracelet around on her wrist. If only she could go back. Her body flopped down on the bare mattress, her eyes focused on the bracelet. A smile played on her lips. She was back at the lake. Her eyes closed, all the stress of the last few days slipping away. Her breathing eased and she let herself be drawn from all the hurt and pain.

Chapter Ten

She came to with a start sometime in the early hours of the morning, her body shivering uncontrollably. Slowly she eased her stiff joints into a sitting position, wincing as her feet dropped down onto the cold floor. Wrapping her arms around her body she tried to ward off the cold that had seeped into her body. Her teeth began to chatter. The room was encased in darkness. An all too familiar feeling of panic began to clutch at her when she suddenly realized where she was. Her heart rate increased. She reached out and placed her hand against the wall, crying out in pain as she got to her feet. Using the wall for support, she hobbled towards the door, stretching her hand out in front of her she began the desperate search for the light switch. A relieved sigh escaped her when her hand finally closed over it. She flicked it on. Her hand flew up to shield her eyes from the glare. She slowly scanned the room wondering, what had bought her here? A dull ache emanated from behind her eyes. She rubbed her temples, trying to ease the relentless pounding in her head. Everything seemed so frightfully familiar. A cold shiver ran up her spine. She walked over to the window, her heart clenched. Her father had built her the little window seat. Many an hour had been spent staring out of this very window. Her leg brushed against an overturned chair. It was the one thing she realized that didn't belong in her room. Her brow creased as she slowly tilted her head to look at the beam above her head. Her eyes widened, and her hand flew to her mouth. Shaking her head slowly from side to side she backed away. The rub mark around the beam was clearly visible. Her body stiffened. He had hanged himself in her room. In her mind she could see him. His body dangling limp, the rope tied firmly around his neck. Her breath caught in her throat. She let out a strangled cry as she staggered back towards the door. She could hear the creaking of the rope as it groaned under his weight. His bulging eyes were now blank and lifeless staring out at her. Her stomach tightened as she shot from the room and stumbled into the bathroom. The contents of her stomach emptied into the bowl. She ran the back of her hand across her mouth. Moving to the sink she turned on the tap and took a big gulp of water then spat it back out. Her stomach contracted again but there was nothing left.

She made her way out into the hallway and headed for the front door. Her hand grabbed at the banister to stop herself falling as she hastily descended the stairs. When she reached the bottom she turned to look at the landing above. Hurriedly she made her way to the front door. Wrenching it open, she staggered out onto the porch slamming it closed behind her. Before she knew it, she was out on the street. When she hit the pavement she broke into a run, visions of her father's body swinging from the beam still raw in her mind. Why had he done it in her room? Had he felt guilty or was he getting back at her for leaving?. She increased her speed, unaware that she was causing more damage to her already battered and bruised feet. Nothing seemed to register except the desperate need to get away. The sunrise was only minutes away, but it did little to ease the cold fear that had crept inside her. The stillness of the empty streets only helped fuel her growing fear. There was no one to save her. She could hear his laboured breathing as he slowly closed in on her. No matter how fast she ran, there was no getting away from him. Her chest heaved as her lungs screamed for air, but she wouldn't let up.

The motel stood in silent semi darkness. She raced to her door and turned the knob. It was locked. She pulled frantically at it as she glanced back over her shoulder. Placing her back against the door, she turned to face the street expecting to see her father appear any minute. Her body tensed like a coiled spring. The driveway remained empty. Slowly she released her breath, giving a little hysterical laugh. "He's dead. He can't hurt you anymore." She let her body slip to the ground, deep sobs wracking her frame. Was it ever going to end? Was she ever going to rid herself of him?

Nancy found her about an hour later sitting propped up against her door. Her legs were drawn up against her chest and her head was resting on her knees. Nancy could hear her mumbling something, but couldn't make sense of what she was saying. Carley startled when Nancy reached out and lightly touched her on the shoulder. "What an earth are you doing out here. You're frozen."
Carley lifted her head and looked up, her puffy swollen eyes round with fear.
"Carley, it's me Nancy, what happened" she said her voice full of concern as she took in Carley's bloodied feet and knees.
"I forgot my, .my... k..k....keyyyy... Carley said through chattering teeth.
Nancy took hold of her arm and drew her to her feet. "Carley, I told you to call me anytime for any reason. Now come on in and let's get you warmed up."

Carley's limbs felt stiff and sore and her feet were throbbing with an unrelenting vengeance. Nancy opened the door and helped Carley inside, sitting her down on a chair. She closed the door behind them then walked into the bathroom and turned on the shower.

"Now come on, into the shower with you. We need to get you warmed up."

Carley went to rise and sank back down on to the chair. The combination of no food, too much alcohol and the numbing cold had taken their toll. Nancy caught hold of her arm and guided her into the bathroom. Helping her undress, she put her under the warm water. Slowly the cold began to ease out of her limbs. She sighed, knowing the cold would never leave her heart. Nothing would ever fix that. She glanced down at the bracelet on her wrist. Not even Dean could fix it this time. She turned off the shower and stepped out glancing at herself in the mirror. She almost didn't recognise the woman looking back at her. Picking up a towel she quickly dried herself off then slipped into the bathrobe from the door. She wrapped it around her body and fastened the tie around her waist. Feeling a little embarrassed about her earlier theatrics, she hobbled back out into the other room.

Nancy was sitting on the chair waiting for her.

Carley smiled, "Thank you, I'm sorry. I didn't mean to put you to any trouble"

She looked down at Carley's feet. "Now, how about we see to those."

Carley glanced down at her feet, they were certainly a mess. "You don't have to. I am quite capable of doing them myself."

Nancy smiled "I'm quite sure you are, but I'm here now, so sit."

Carley sat down on the chair opposite, flinching as Nancy gently picked up one of her feet and placed it on her lap. She liked that Nancy didn't try to make conversation or ask her any questions, she just worked away quietly, applying cream and plasters to the cuts and abrasions. Carley gulped back her tears. No one had cared for her this much in a very long time. When Nancy had finished tending to the first foot, she carefully placed it back on the floor and picked up the next one. Carley's eyes met hers. "Thank you."

Nancy smiled "Anytime lovey, we all need a bit of help now and again. We just need to know when to ask for it."

A lump formed in Carley's throat. Nancy was absolutely right. Here she was thinking she could do everything herself, when in reality she couldn't. She certainly couldn't do the house by herself and she hadn't really managed her father's funeral on her own either. And and now this. Nancy finished tending to all her cuts and rose up off the chair. She gave Carley a warm smile. "There, all done. Now I know it's probably none of my business but if you ever need to talk, my door is always open." She patted Carley's shoulder "You take care now."

Carley watched her leave then hobbled over to the door and closed it. Her body gave a little shiver. She was alone again. The sooner she could get rid of that damned house the better. This town held far too many painful memories for her liking. All she wanted was to move on with her life and leave all this behind. She laughed out loud. What life? She still had no idea what she wanted to do. Then there was Dean. He just didn't seem to fit in anywhere. He had once been a very big part of her life. A part she now realized had been one of the better times of her life. No man had ever made her feel the way he did. Hobbling back into the bedroom she threw herself down on the bed. Why did her life always have to be so damn complicated?

Chapter Eleven

Two days had passed since she had run from the house. Nancy had loaned her a hammer so she could nail the board back over the window, but she hadn't dare enter. Today she was going to make an effort and start on the garden. Hoping that being around there might give her the courage she needed to go inside. Pulling the door closed on her motel room she found herself smiling for the first time in days. The sun was shining, the birds were singing and it looked as though it was going to be an absolutely glorious day. Summer had always been her favourite time of year and it never failed to remind her of her mother bent over, tending her garden. What she wouldn't do to hear the comforting sound of her mother's laughter just once more.

When she arrived, she made her way around to the side of the house and pulled out the few garden tools that she knew Dean had been kind enough to stow there. She still didn't know what had caused her to be so careless. Her eyes turned to the large burnt ring on the lawn and the heap of burned timber that used to be the garden shed. Dragging the tools around to the front of the house, she set them down on the lawn. Picking up the spade she dug it into the dirt jamming her foot down on it as she tried to break through the rock hard surface. After a few more tries she threw the spade down on the ground. Feeling defeated, she walked over to the garden and began pulling out what she hoped were weeds. There were still a few of her mother's plants struggling for survival. With the greatest of care she cleared around them. They were in pretty bad shape and she wasn't sure they'd survive, but at least she had tried.

As she worked she became acutely aware of the silent presence of the house in the background. She shivered at the thought of having to re-enter it. For the next two hours she worked feverishly, determined to at least make some progress towards getting the house ready for sale. The sun beat down relentlessly and the temperature slowly began to climb. She wiped the sweat from her brow. By midday all her energy and enthusiasm had been drained, and exhausted she collapsed down onto the grass under the tree, its thick canopy giving her instant relief from the sun's harsh rays. She fanned herself with an old newspaper that she had found in the letter box but it did little to alleviate her discomfort. Flopping onto her back she stared up into the branches. Part of the rope that had held her childhood swing was still visible. Over the years it had been slowly swallowed by the bark and was now almost part of the tree. As she thought back to her childhood, images of the lake sprang to mind. It had been their secret place that no one else knew about. She hurriedly got to her feet, the need to see it now burning strongly within her. It had been a place to forget all her worries and simply be a child. A frown crossed her brow. Truthfully, it had been Dean who had made those days so special. She had loved him without question but the thought of being in love with him had never crossed her mind. Without a second thought she strode off in the direction of the lake. What must it have been like for him? To have someone you loved disappear and you not know where or why? If he had done the same to her she would never have forgiven him. Yet here he was, back in her life as if nothing had happened.

She hesitated when she reached the path that led out to the lake. Her body stiffened. Did she really want to look back into her past? It took her all her courage not to turn around and head back the way she had come. The pull was strong and she knew in her heart that she had to see it one last time. Warily she made her way along the path. Would it hold the same appeal as it had all those years ago? Her breath caught in her throat as the lake appeared before her. It looked just as she remembered it, seemingly undisturbed by the passing years. Her eyes moistened. Both she and Dean had spent most of that last summer out here. It should have been a time for young love and experimentation instead all she had felt was fear and confusion. Tears trickled down her cheek. Her trust in him had been broken the moment he had kissed her and tried to place his hand on her breast. He had been the only one she felt she could trust, yet in that one instant he had hurt her more than he would ever know. That summer had quickly turned into one of the darkest times in her life. Dean had wanted something from her that she couldn't give. Deep down, she had always known that one day she would somehow find the strength to escape from her father's abuse but had never imagined having to run from Dean.

She stood watching as a small ripple rolled out across the lake's glass like surface. Dare she enter its depths and revisit her past? Her feet moved closer to the edge of the bank. She could almost feel the cold clear water gliding over her heated skin. Her eyes remained locked on the lake as she slipped her feet out of her shoes. Gripping the hem of her shirt she pulled it up her body and off over her head. Her body gave a little shiver as she dropped it to the ground. Now bare to the waist she gently eased the zip down on her shorts, sliding them down her legs she stepped out of them. A cool breeze played across her skin. Slipping her fingers inside the elastic of her underwear she rolled them down her legs and placed them on top of her clothing. Drawing in a deep calming breath, she took the last tentative step towards the water's edge. She stood there enjoying the freedom. So many years had been wasted making other people happy, now it was her turn. In one graceful movement she sprang off the bank and dived into the crystal clear water. Only the slightest of ripples broke the surface as she entered its depths. When her head broke the surface, she gave a childish little giggle. There was nothing like a refreshing dip to clear a troubled mind. Her head dropped back into the water. She floated on her back, aimlessly staring up at the brilliant blue cloudless sky above. Her hands glided gently back and forth across the surface of the water as she slowly made her way to the centre of the lake. Silence surrounded her. Her thoughts began to drift. What would her life have been like had she stayed? Would she be living out here with him? She gave a little forced laugh. In her experience, dreams very rarely come true and she was certain they wouldn't have for her.

Time slowly slipped by. Giving a sigh, she reluctantly turned for shore. It was nice being out here but without him it didn't feel quite the same. As she reached the shallows she let her feet drop to the lake bed. Her mind travelled back over the last few days. A lot had happened and it was still hard for her to get her head around it all. Slowly she began to make her way to the shore. Her body began to relax for the first time in days as she tilted her face up to absorb the sun's rays. A smile touched her lips as she trailed her finger tips across the surface of the water. Maybe it was possible, to carve out a new life for herself and finally put all the hurt behind her. A sudden movement caught her eye.

She gave a startled gasp as her eyes met with his. Her arms moved to cover her naked breasts. Being naked in front of men wasn't something that would normally bother her, but with him it felt wrong.

"What the hell..., you scared the shit out of me."

He gave her an apologetic grin, "Sorry, I didn't realize anybody was here" he replied leaning back against the tree, his eyes still firmly fixed on her.

The cool water lapped at her waist. A small quiver ran up her spine. She groaned inwardly. Of all the people to come across her, did it have to be him?

Her eyes narrowed "What the hell do you think you're looking at?"

He let a few seconds pass before he answered, "Do you honestly want me to answer that?"

She fixed him with a cold stare. "What are you doing here?"

He shifted position, his body tensing. "I was about to ask you the same thing."

She rolled her eyes. "Taking a swim, what does it look like?"

The corner of his eyes crinkled as he stifled a grin, "I can see that..."

Her eyes narrowed as a cold shiver ran up her spine. "If you don't mind, I would like to get out."

His eyes darkened. "No one's stopping you."

If it was a battle of wills he would surely lose. She dropped her arms to her sides.

He shifted position, the cocky smile dropping from his face. Giving herself an imaginary pat on the back she began to make her way to shore.

Unable to draw his gaze away, his eyes followed her.

She glanced up at him through her long thick lashes. "Were you spying on me?"

He felt himself harden, "If you choose to swim... naked," he let his eyes travel her body. "On private property, you should be prepared for the possibility that you might get caught."

Her nipples peaked under his intense stare. "Private... property...?," she stammered, "but we..., she hesitated. "But I've always swum here." He jaw clenched, *It was "we", Carley. We used to swim here.* He pushed away from the tree but couldn't seem to draw his eyes away. This had been a big mistake on his part and he was now paying for it. "It sold, about two years ago," he said rather abruptly. Carley felt a small tug on her heart. This had been their place, and now it belonged to someone else. She gave a defeated sigh. "And how could I have possibly have known that?" she replied as she reached the shore, now feeling very conscious of her nakedness. Snatching a piece of clothing from the ground, she began to hurriedly dress, fully aware of his eyes still upon her. She glanced over at him and he caught her eye. "There is a sign on the driveway."

Why did he have to look so damn sexy standing there in his worn low slung jeans and collared shirt? The fact that the shirt hung open, giving her a good view of his sculptured chest and toned abdomen only seemed to frustrate her all the more. Her brow creased.

"What sign," she spat suddenly noticing his bare feet. He smiled as he watched her struggling to pull her shorts up her wet legs.

"There's a' Trespass' sign."

She stopped what she was doing, and looked over at him, "I didn't see any trespass sign. Anyway, doesn't that make you a trespasser too?" He drew his eyebrows together. "Not really."

Why was he being so damned infuriating? She yanked her shorts up the rest of the way and zipped them up. Why didn't he just leave and end this torture? "So why is it that I'm trespassing and you're not?" she asked, trying to ignore the warm feeling growing deep inside her.

He gave her a stupid lopsided grin, "I've known the owner for years. Don't worry, I'm pretty sure he wouldn't mind you swimming naked in his lake....," he paused letting his eyes roam her body. "I mean what man in his right mind would?"

She glared at him. "And I suppose you just happened to be passing," she replied, trying to drag her top down over her damp body. "Something like that," he replied, grinning as he watched her struggling with it. "You sure you don't need a hand with that?"

"No thank you" she hissed, yanking it the rest of the way down. She gave him a forced grin. "Well, be sure to give the owner my sincere apologies and tell him that I won't TRESPASS..., again won't you?."

He smiled. "There's no need; he already knows."

She gave a sudden gasp. "You own it don't you?" she asked slipping her feet into her sandals.

He nodded, "I bought it a few years back."

Her eyes turned to the lake. "Why?"

He frowned, *why! Didn't she remember? It had been their dream.* "Because... I like it here."

It was her turn to frown. He actually owned it. He had brought their dream to life. Her heart clenched, "Well, you can be sure I won't bother you again. After all, I wouldn't want to TRESPASS..., now would I?"

He stood staring at her in silence. It was going exactly how he had hoped it would.

Her eyes narrowed "So did you enjoy the show?"

He looked into her eyes and she saw a flicker of the hurt she had inflicted on him all those years ago. A pang of guilt shot through her. She moved toward him and felt her heart rate quicken. Having never felt the power of sexual attraction she wasn't sure she liked it. His eyes drifted to where her taut nipples pressed invitingly against the thin damp fabric of her shirt. She smiled inwardly when she saw his body stiffen. At least he was finding this just as uncomfortable as she was.

His eyes moved to hers. A pink tinge crept into her cheeks. It was hard for her to be this close to him and her body not betray her. His body was taut with tension as his focus shifted to those beautiful pouty lips. It took all his restraint not to reach and capture them in his. He took a deep sobering breath. Was he really stupid enough to risk being rejected all over again? His body was saying yes, but his head was saying no. Before he could move forward he needed to know the answer to the one question which had been plaguing him for years. Why? He wanted to ask her, but was he really ready for the answer? His eyes sought hers. She had already managed to ignite a fire deep down inside him. One he knew only she could extinguish. His body tensed as he noticed the bracelet encircling her left wrist. His heart gave a sudden lurch and began to hammer away wildly in his chest. What did it all mean? Was it possible that she still had feelings for him? He took a couple of deep breaths. What man in his right mind wouldn't want her? To him she was the picture of perfection. He struggled with the sudden need to have her. Did he really need to know why? Was it worth running the risk of losing her again? She was back; wasn't that all that mattered? Her thick black lashes blinked slowly across her bright blue eyes. A hint of a smile touched her lips. She was more beautiful than any woman he had ever seen and he had seen his fair share. Her skin was smooth and flawless tanned to the colour of coffee cream accentuating the bright blue of her large almond shaped eyes. Her soft pink lips, their colour now heightened by the cool water seemed to pout invitingly at him. His eyes locked on the small scar running across one of her eyebrows. He could still remember the day she had got it. All he needed was a small sign that the Carley he had grown to love so long ago was still in there somewhere. His fists clenched, why was he putting himself through this? He already knew the answer, because he still loved her.

It took all her willpower not to reach out and trace her finger along his strong jaw line. There was evidence of a missed shave. A look she had always found rather appealing. His lips were invitingly full and his eyes, while still green, seemed darker and more volatile than she remembered only days before. As if they were warning her that she was now treading on dangerous ground. An uncomfortable silence fell between them, broken only by the harshness of their breathing. Both of them were now balanced on the edge of restraint. Neither of them daring to take the next step, knowing full well there would be no turning back. She cursed silently to herself. How had she let herself get into this situation? What had she hoped to achieve? The happily ever after she had always dreamed of? As if that was likely to happen! An invisible line had been drawn between them that neither of them were willing to cross. She suddenly felt so alone that tears began to sting the back of her eyes. This could only lead to more heartache. Coming here had been a huge mistake on her part. Her eyes dropped to the ground. She could never give him the answers he so desperately needed.

He cursed silently. Why couldn't he think of anything to say? Seeing the bracelet had given him a little hope, but he wasn't about to lay his heart out there for her to trample all over. He had hoped for some sort of explanation. She had put him through so much torment, didn't he at least deserved that? Without a second's hesitation he reached up and gently brushed his finger across her scar. She let out a startled gasp, leaping away from him. He dropped his hand and took a step back. When would he learn that things had changed? As she stood there staring wide eyed she finally saw the hurt she had inflicted on him all those year ago. Why had she let it get this far? He didn't deserve to be treated like this. For some reason, every time she was around him all her common sense seemed to fly out the window. She glanced up at him, her eyes moist. His eyes burned intently into hers. Silence fell around them.

"I can't believe you bought our lake," she offered, desperately trying to fill the void between them.

He cringed inwardly," *our lake,*". It was like a red-hot poker to his heart. He nodded, the deep sadness now evident in his eyes. "I had always hoped..., that someday..., you'd come back. But it's obvious that you don't want to be here. Do you?"

What was she suppose to say? If she said yes, she knew it would be a lie. Tears began to trickle down her face, "I..., I just don't. Dean..., I'm sorry for everything. I really didn't mean this to happen. I didn't want to hurt you" she said, taking a step towards him

"Don't" he snapped, stepping back.

Her body stiffened. His words were like a slap in the face. He had never spoken to her that way, ever.

He stood for a minute, his eyes locked on hers, "Carley. Why did you leave me?"

Carley dropped her eyes to the ground. Even though she knew how much she had hurt him, she still couldn't bring herself to tell him. She didn't want him to know all the sordid details of her past. Not him. She didn't need his pity. All she wanted was to put her past behind her and move on with her life. Her feet shuffled in the loose gravel and she found herself unable to look him in the eye. If she could just think of something to say. Anything would be better than the silence now hanging between them. She shook her head slowly from side to side. There was nothing she was willing to say that could take away the damage she had already inflicted. Dean shoved his clenched fists deep into his pockets. Turning on his heel he stalked away. Carley watched him go, wanting nothing more than to call him back and explain. A long sigh escaped her lips.

"What you don't know won't hurt you." She whispered quietly to herself as she watched him disappear down the path. Tears trickled down her cheeks. The best thing she could do for Dean right now was to get out of his life for good. As she headed up the driveway, she dared to take one last look back.

"Goodbye Dean. I really hope you find the happiness you are looking for and that someday you can find it in your heart to forgive me."

Dean stormed into the house kicking over a chair as he passed.

That woman was the most frustrating and infuriating person he had ever had the pleasure of knowing. She had the ability to trigger every emotion he possessed in a matter of minutes. He strode to the fridge, grabbed four beers and headed off down to the lake edge. Anger raged through him. Why? Why couldn't she tell him? What was she so damn afraid of? His heart clenched. He had seen that frightened look in her eyes once before. It was the day she had fled from his life. Now she was back, causing his heart to ache all over again. He unscrewed the top of the bottle and took a long swig. He hated that she could trigger the old feelings so easily. She had the ability to set his body on fire one minute and infuriate him beyond words the next. He raised the bottle to his lips. And what was with the bracelet? Why would she want to wear it if he meant nothing to her? As he looked out over the lake he thought of how she had stood unashamedly naked before him. He felt himself harden. The Carley he had known would never have done that. He tossed the empty bottle down on the grass and reached for another. As children they had sat on the bank of this very lake dreaming of a future together. He had bought it hoping that one day she might return and share it with him. Now he saw what a fool he had been. She would leave, and he would be left with nothing but fading images. He slumped back down onto the grass. If he couldn't have her then he was probably destined to be alone. There wasn't another woman alive that could stir his emotions like she could. He had always liked a challenge, which was why he had become a fireman. The problem was, he also liked to be challenged in his personal life too. Up until now, he had not found a woman capable of doing that. Now the one woman he felt could, was about to exit his life for the second time.

Chapter Twelve

Carley woke from a dream filled sleep feeling tired and irritable. Getting a decent night's sleep seemed to be a thing of the past. The emotions Dean had stirred in her were still very much on her mind. Just thinking about him was enough to start her dreaming of another life; one that she knew she had no right to. The past few days had been spent going over the scene at the lake. In her heart she knew he deserved to know the truth. Even after all this time the thought of delving into the past had her stomach twisted in knots. For twelve years she had managed to keep her secret. She gave a long sigh. It was time to let it go. What if she had pushed him too far? Even Dean had to have a breaking point. After their little encounter at the lake she didn't feel it would be in her best interest to simply stroll out there without first testing the waters. She needed somewhere public, a place where he would have no choice but to listen.

An hour and a half later she was walking up the driveway to the fire station, with a twelve pack of beer in one hand and a box of doughnuts in the other. She stopped just short of the station house. What would he think of her turning up here? There was only one way to find out she thought, giving a shrug. At least here, he would have to be civil and at the very least give her a chance to say what it was she had come to say. Her body gave a little shiver as she recalled the way he had looked at her. It had frightened her to know that the kind, patient young boy she once knew was now a man filled with anger that was directed at her. He wasn't a violent man, of that she was sure but she had learnt from experience that men aren't always as they first appeared. Taking a deep a breath she marched up the driveway to the door marked office. The door stood open. She stepped inside. The room was empty; her chest tightened as she moved towards the door which led to the engine house. A frightened squeal escaped her when a gruff stocky looking man suddenly appeared in front of her. He positioned himself between her and the firehouse, barring her way.

"You're not allowed in there," he grumbled, indicating towards the desk. "You should have rung the bell."

Her hand shook as she held the beer in front of her like some sort of peace offering. "I'm sorry..., I didn't know."

The man gave an impatient huff. "So what was it you were wanting?"

"Umm..., I wanted to drop these off..., to say thanks for rescuing me and putting out the fire in my back yard..., the other day."

His brow creased as he snatched the beers and doughnuts from her hands, giving her a quick going over with his eyes. His disapproval of her choice of dress was obvious. "I'll be sure to let the boys know you dropped by."

Her brow furrowed "Oh, right," she replied, feeling as though she had been rather hastily dismissed. At a loss as to what to do next, she turned to leave and nearly bumped into another man who had come up behind her.

A smile crossed her face "You were there at the fire in my back yard."
He smiled "That I was. So what is it we can we do for you?"
She gave him a wide confident smile nodding her head towards the beer
and doughnuts. "I bought a little something, just to say thanks and
apologise for all the trouble I caused."
He grinned causing soft crinkles to appear at the corner of his eyes and
mouth "It weren't no bother. You weren't to know."
The first man rolled his eyes and gave a loud humph, then turned and
left with the beer and doughnuts in hand. Two more men appeared at
the other end of the station house and quickly made their way over to
where Carley was standing. To her disappointment neither of them was
Dean. She had envisaged walking in here and running into him as soon
as she stepped through the door.
One of them grinned as he approached her, "I remember you. You were
the one that set fire to your back yard.
"That would be me" she replied, feeling rather foolish. "I'm really sorry
about that."
His eyes slowly travelled the length of her body "T'was my pleasure."
She ignored the bold scan of her frame and smiled sweetly.
"I was just wondering if the fireman who dragged me away from the
fire is here...? I would like the chance to thank him..., personally" she
asked, trying to sound casual even though her nerves were already in
tatters.
The two men elbowed each other and grinned. "You can thank me
personally instead if you like" replied one of them.
She had to restrain herself from giving a sharp rebuttal; instead she
chose to simply roll her eyes.
The man she had recognized from the fire turned to glare at them
"Behave yourselves you two." He gave a sigh "Idiots" he mumbled
under his breath. He turned back to Carley and gave her a warm smile.
"Don't mind them" he turned to glare at them "They seem to have
forgotten their manners. I'm afraid Dean's not in yet but he will be here

shortly if you'd like to wait."

She hesitated. Now she was here she wasn't sure if she wanted to see him. "Um... I suppose I should..., that's if you don't mind."

"As if" whispered one of the other men.

"You can wait in here if you like," he said gesturing to what looked like their dining room.

She gave him a dazzling smile "That would be great, thanks." Her eyebrows rose as the three of them followed her into the room. He pulled out a chair for her. She sat down, thanking him. Then to her surprise all three of them pulled up chairs and sat down. Even the grumpy one who she had met at the door came to join them, carrying the box of doughnuts. Silence filled the room she shifted in her seat, feeling all four pairs of eyes resting on her.

"I'm Carley, please feel free to help yourselves to the doughnuts," she said breaking the silence.

The grumpy one who was now sitting beside her, grabbed for a doughnut, she smiled at him.

"So what's your name?"

Silence filled the room. He didn't even bother to acknowledge that she had spoken.

"Oh don't mind him, he doesn't like women much, especially pretty ones" said the man who had offered her a seat. He shook his head. "It's a long story. We call him Smiley for reasons you might have already guessed."

She glanced over at him again. He was a solidly built man with a fairly pronounced pot belly. A long straggly beard covered the bottom half of his face. Remnants of the demolished doughnut could be seen sitting amongst his whiskers. He suddenly turned and gave her a cold hard stare. A shiver ran up her spine. His eyes were almost black, his lips set in a hard line. She tore her eyes away but could feel his eyes boring into her.

"Honestly, don't mind him, he's harmless really."

She turned her focus back to the man that had shown her into the room and was again met with a warm smile. Her body began to relax. "They call me Smokey."

She gave him a puzzled look "Smokey?"

"Most of us have nicknames, mine came about due to getting myself trapped in a burning building."

Carley gave him a horrified look.

He smiled. "By the time the guys finally got me out. I was literally smoking."

They all laughed but Carley found it hard to see the funny side. Smokey was probably the better-looking one out of the group. She guessed him to be in his early thirties. He had big solid looking arms and shoulders. His dark hair was cut short against his scalp and his skin was deeply tanned. Beautiful ice blue eyes smiled right along with him. She instantly felt at ease in his company.

At that moment two more men strolled through the door "So what's going on here then? Look, they've been holding out on us." Smokey looked up at them "Sorry guys, we should have called you. This is Carley, she's waiting to see Dean. She was nice enough to bring us beer and doughnuts."

Both of them moved into the room, each pulling up a chair and making sure to grab a doughnut each. Carley relaxed a little more. Men were easy to handle and this lot, all except one seemed like a really nice bunch of guys. She casually crossed one slender thigh over the other noticing every single pair of eyes take in that one simple movement. Men were so predictable. The young man sitting at the far end caught her eye she gave him a warm smile.

"And what's your name?"

"E...van" he replied blushing. "They don't have a nickname for me yet. I'm only new and haven't done anything stupid yet."

Laughter erupted around the room. The man next to him slapped him on the back.

"Don't worry, your time will come."

He glanced up at Carley and his blush deepened.

"Well, it's very nice to meet you Evan." He looked far too young to be a firefighter. With his slim boyish build, fine blonde hair and large hazel eyes he could have passed for sixteen. Carley's eyes moved to the next man.

He gave her a wide cheesy grin "They call me Spider."

The man next to him dug him in the ribs "Behave yourself." Spider grinned "Always."

She could tell just by looking at him that he was one she would have to watch. He was fit and lean and he wore his brown hair a little longer than the rest of the men in the room. His startling green eyes locked on hers.

"It's a pleasure to meet you, Spider."

He grinned, "Believe me, the pleasure's all mine.

The man next to him spoke "Jeez Spider, give it a rest. Don't mind him he thinks he's god's gift to all woman."

Spiders put on a hurt look, Carley laughed.

"So why is he called Spider?'"

"It's because he shoots up the ladders like a freaking spider, quick as that. He has even been known to shimmy up the side of buildings if the need arises. And then, there is the fact that a lot of women seem to get caught in his web."

A playful glint appeared in Spider's eyes.

Yes, she knew his type, all false bravado and no real depth. Her eyes moved to the next man.

He smiled sheepishly "They call me Wing nut on account of me ears" he said flicking the tips of his ears.

They all laughed. He wasn't what you would call attractive. His face was long and narrow, he had big teeth set into a decidedly small mouth and a long slightly crooked nose. His body was lean but he didn't seem to carry the same muscular fitness that Spider's did. Finally she turned to the last man.

"I'm Rowdy" he said quietly.

She smiled. He was a meek sort of man of medium build and almost completely bald. When he eventually smiled, Carley noticed he had two teeth missing in the front. She was now curious as to whether Dean had a nickname and if so what it would be.

Dean entered the station house quickly, making his way towards the voices. His brow creased. So this was how they passed the time when he wasn't here. A quick glance at the engines told him that they still hadn't been washed. Giving an exasperated sigh he stalked over to the dining room, his already dark mood darkening even further. He didn't like slackers on his team. He needed to be able to trust then to complete a simple task. He rounded the doorway.

"What's going on here, those...," He came to an abrupt halt, his eyes widening in surprise. His body tensed as he struggled to contain the jealousy flaring up inside him. How dare she come in here dressed like that. He pushed his hand through his hair. His jaw tightened as he turned his cold hard stare on her. Was she purposely trying to make his life a living hell? Her eyes met his. She let out a small gasp and shot to her feet knocking over the chair, which crashed noisily to the floor. The room fell silent. They stood staring at each other, oblivious to the looks they were getting from everyone around them. One by one the men began to exit the room. A lump formed in her throat. They were leaving her alone with him. She stood motionless held by his stare. Everything she had intended to say slipped from her mind. The last man disappeared out the door and a tense silence filled the room. Her eyes dropped to the table as she traced the grain with her finger.

"What are you doing here?" he snapped.

She looked up at him his eyes were blazing with anger. "I... I thought....," she hesitated.

His eyes narrowed, "You thought what, that you could come in here and humiliate me in front of my workmates? I don't like games Carley. You had no right to come here..." He let his eyes travel her body taking in the short skirt and body hugging tee-shirt, "especially dressed like that." Tears pricked the back of her eyes. Why was he being so cruel? She hadn't done anything wrong.

Her back bristled as her eyes met his in a defiant glare. Drawing herself up to her full height she squared her shoulders. "Who do you think you are?" She placed her hands on her hips. "I can wear anything I damn well please! And for your information I didn't come here for you." His mouth dropped open. "If you had taken the time to ask I would have told you that I came to say thanks."

His brow creased.

She rolled her eyes, "for the fire thing." She said as she bent to pick up the chair, setting it on its feet. "If that's alright with you?"

Her eyes held his in a fierce gaze.

He stood speechless.

"Well, say something."

His body tensed. She was right he had over reacted. His eyes softened, "Carley, I'm sorry, I didn't realise."

She gritted her teeth, knowing she needed to get away and fast. "I don't know why I bothered" she muttered as she stalked across the room towards the door.

He stepped in front of her.

She glanced up at him. "Let me past."

He reached out and placed his hand on her arm. "Carley... please... I'm sorry."

Her eyes widened at his touch. She snatched her arm away. She couldn't risk letting him touch her, not now when she was feeling so fragile and could so easily give in to temptation.

Her voice softened. "I didn't come here for a fight," She hesitated. "Oh to hell with it, it wasn't just to drop off the damn beer and doughnuts either."

His eyebrows shot up "It wasn't?"

She gave him a half hearted smile, "I came to see you."

"You did."

"I hurt you. I know that. And to be honest I don't know why you even want to speak to me."

"Carley, it's okay really."

Her eyes turned to his "It's not okay and you damn well know it. I owe you an explanation."

"Carley you don't have to do this, honestly. I should never have pushed it."

Tears pricked the back of her eyes. "I should have told you a long time ago." Tear welled up behind her lashes. "I'm truly sorry... for everything."

He took a step closer.

Her breath caught in her throat as she tilted her face up to his, her eyes momentarily lingering on his lips. His look intensified sending a small quiver up her spine.

"Dean, I need to explain but not now, not here."

His eyes travelled the face he had known so many years ago. It was plain to see she was scared, but scared of what... him?"

Her eyes blinked slowly "Could we meet somewhere and talk?"

He was still a little shocked. Was she actually going to tell him, after all this time?

"Dean, did you hear me?"

"Oh... right. When?"

Carley thought about it for a minute. "What about on your next day off?"

"I suppose..., but that's not till Sunday."

"Well if it's okay with you, I'll come out to your place on Sunday."

He hesitated. "That would be okay, I guess" he replied, now unsure how he was going to manage to wait until then.

Carley moved closer to the door. "So, Sunday it is then."

Dean didn't move, effectively blocking her exit.

He smiled down at her. "I'm sorry if I came on a bit strong. You took me by surprise..., I wasn't expecting...."

She smiled up at him, fighting against the temptation to reach up and place her lips against his. Their bodies were now only inches apart. He had the freshly showered smell of soap on him. His eyes darkened. Suddenly she came to her senses; stepping to one side she quickly pushed passed him. By the time she reached the exterior door her heart was racing. The sunlight hit her face. She paused for a second, momentarily blinded and drew in a deep breath. That had been too damn close for comfort. Why did she keep putting herself into these situations? If she kept this up she would be ripping his clothes off right here in the car park. She started to make her way down the drive. "Carley, wait," she turned to see Dean following her down the drive. She gave a small groan, drawing to a stop.

He smiled as he approached her, "I just wanted to make sure you're okay."

An exasperated sigh escaped her lips. "Yes, like I've said so many times before, I'm fine."

He smiled. "Okay, okay I get it I won't ask again. So I'll see you on Sunday then?."

She nodded "Look I've got to go," she said turning and hurrying down the drive not daring to look back. Tears rolled down her cheeks; it was something she seemed to be doing rather a lot lately.

He frowned as he watched her leave wondering what it could be that she had to tell him. Shoving his hands into his pockets he headed back into the station. As he entered, he felt several pairs of eyes watching him.

"None of your damn business" he announced angrily, "So don't even bother asking" The men looked around at each other and shrugged their shoulders, knowing there was no point in pressing it.

As she walked back to the Motel, she wondered how she was going to manage to wait until Sunday; three whole days of torture. He had certainly triggered some very powerful emotions in her, which seemed to run rampant whenever he was near. What was it about him that turned her into a wanton hussy? Her brow creased, and why had she never experienced anything like it before? What would his reaction be when she finally told him? Would he be repulsed by her, and not want anything to do with her... or... would he..? A smile creased her lips. Hmm... she let out a sudden gasp. No! God no! How could she even think it, she wasn't going to go down that road, she didn't want anything from him. All she needed was to rid herself of the guilt and make a fresh start as far away from this town as possible. He didn't need to know how she had earned a living; that was her business and no one else's. It was also the very reason she could never let anything happen between them, no matter how strong the attraction.

Chapter Thirteen

For the next three days she tried to keep herself busy. Nancy had been kind enough to go with her to the house. It had still been very difficult for her enter and even now she hated going in there, but it was something which had to be done. Luckily she found her mind constantly focused elsewhere. Worrying about how she was going to tell him and what his reaction would be. She tried to push the thoughts from her mind but nothing seemed to work. Maybe it would have been better if she had simply left. She rubbed her aching forehead. This certainly wasn't the right town for her to try and make a fresh start in. There were too many bad memories and way too much uncertainty for her liking. If she could just put some distance between her and Dean, hopefully things would simply fizzle out and they could both move on with their lives. Staying here wouldn't be a move forward, it would be more like a huge step backwards. It would be in the best interests of both of them to leave their past in the past, where it belonged.

As Sunday approached, the tension began to mount. Thoughts of jumping on the next bus and leaving town had grown more appealing by the day. The only thing holding her back was knowing how much it would hurt him. She couldn't. No, she wouldn't do that to him again. Letting out a long sigh, she resigned herself to the fact that seeing him once more had changed everything. The option to leave had come and gone, and all she had to look forward to now was more heartache.

She felt herself teetering on the brink of sanity. The fact that she hadn't slept properly in two days wasn't helping. Her appetite was almost nonexistent and she couldn't stop thinking about him day or night. By the time Sunday arrived, her nerves were in tatters, she had lost weight and she looked tired and drawn. Glancing in the mirror she groaned, hardly recognising the person staring back at her. Snatching up her makeup she began dabbing it under her eyes trying to disguise the dark circles that now seemed a permanent feature. There was a slight throbbing at her temples. With a loud groan, she tossed the compact into the sink. Glancing over at the clock, she knew she couldn't prolong it any longer. It was either now or never.

Setting a brisk pace, she quickly made her way up the main street oblivious to the stares she was receiving from the town's people. All she could think about was what lay ahead. Any minute now she was expecting the small amount of courage she had managed to muster to simply evaporate. The tension in her body kept building. Her steps faltered as she turned onto the gravel road that led out to his house. Hadn't she suffered enough? Why was she torturing herself by having to relive it all over again? Her pace slowed and she almost turned back, but visions of the hurt look on Dean's face prompted her to keep moving forward. She needed to do this; if not for Dean, for herself. Her brow creased. Dean had always been there for her in the past and she hoped that now wouldn't be any different. Counting her steps aloud she pushed on, trying to distract herself from what lay ahead. It wasn't until the lake came into view that the tension really started to mount. Her stomach made a loud gurgling sound. 'Not now', she thought to herself, 'please not now'. She drew to a halt, and took a long deep breath. "Get a grip" she mumbled to herself, forcing herself to push on. The sunlight glistened off the lake's calm clear surface. A family of ducks were slowly making their way along the bank. One of the adult ducks kept dipping under the water, searching for food as the ducklings waited patiently on the surface for her return. The lake had always had a calming effect on her. It had been her safe place... their safe place. Her eyes were suddenly drawn to a figure moving through the water. She came to an abrupt halt and leaned over feeling as though she were about to vomit. Her heart rate accelerated. Did she even have the strength to do this? Taking a deep breath she tried to calm herself as she watched him move through the water. Would he be there for her? Would he understand why she had to leave? Righting herself she began to walk still clutching at her stomach. She had to believe he would. A line of tree's sprung up between her and the lake. Unable to resist, she peered through the trees periodically to watch him as she made her way towards the house. He reached the far side of the lake and disappeared momentarily under the water only to re-surface again, heading back the way he had come. He made swimming look so effortless. He was a strong powerful swimmer and if memory served her right always had been. Her pace slowed as she drew to a stop behind the last group of trees. His house lay just around the corner. She turned to watch him as he reached the bank knowing she wasn't ready to be alone with him.

His feet hit the lake bed and he rose to his feet, the water trickling off his shoulders and down his back, glistening off his deeply bronzed skin. Her eyes were drawn to him. Suddenly she let out a stifled gasp when she saw that he was naked. Her body gave a little quiver and he was... beautiful as she had known he would be. Her lips turned up at the corners as she took in his strong muscular frame, drinking him in as he stood towelling himself off. Her hand went to her throat, her fingers trailed softly down over her collar bone. Her lips parted ever so slightly. She shifted her position, careful not to alert him of her presence. Her heart began to pound against her chest as her tongue slowly licked across her lips. She had never wanted anything as much as she wanted him right now. If things had been different maybe she would have had the courage to step out from behind the tree and surprise him, as he'd done to her. She bit down hard on her bottom lip as her eyes hungrily devoured his body, taking in the defined contours of his well developed chest and shoulders. His trim waist, narrow hips, and that well defined "V" that lead straight to, she smiled, an impressive set of equipment. A small quiver ran up her body as she thought about the strength and power his body must possess. A warm sensation began to form deep down in the pit of her stomach. Was this how it felt to want someone so badly it hurt? She sighed. Most of the men she had been with had been middle aged, married and a bit podgy around the middle; nothing like the magnificent specimen now standing before her.

He finished drying himself and slung the towel around his hips. Carley leant back against the tree and closed her eyes. Drawing in a couple of deep breaths, she tried to get her thoughts in order. "Are you coming in?"
Her eyes flew open, 'god, no'. Her heart began to race. He had someone else here with him. Her stomach clenched, how could've she been so stupid? Of course he did, look at him. She peeked around the tree and let out another startled gasp when his eyes met hers.
He grinned, "When you're ready. I'll go and put on some coffee," he said, as he turned and walked inside.

She slapped her forehead with the palm of her hand three times "Idiot, idiot, idiot," then let out a long tortured groan. Had he known she was there all along? Now what was she suppose to do? She couldn't very well leave. If she did, how would she ever be able to face him again? No. It was now or never. She would just have to swallow her pride. If she didn't, it would only make her look even more ridiculous than she already felt. Taking a deep breath, she stepped out from behind the tree and slowly made her way up onto the porch. She hesitated at the doorway.

"Come in. You up for a cup of coffee?"

She stepped through the doorway and cautiously made her way to what she presumed was the kitchen. Her breath caught in her throat as she rounded the corner. He was standing at the counter with his back to her, the towel sitting low on his hips.

"Ah... y...yes ...please, a little milk and one sugar," she stammered instantly struck by the raw masculinity of him. Her eyes were drawn to his broad muscular back and shoulders. She sucked in another deep breath, as her eyes took in his firm tight buttocks wrapped in the towel. Her body quivered as she slowly backed out of the room. Knowing he was still naked underneath the towel nearly had her heading for the door. The day was quickly escalating out of control. Her heart rate began to accelerate, and she could already feel the annoying pink tinge creeping on to her cheeks. It was unsettling for her to feel at such a disadvantage. Suddenly she had turned into a bumbling, stuttering idiot and she hated it.

He walked through the doorway from the kitchen giving her a beautiful big cheerful smile "Hello."

"Hi" she replied blushing.

"I'm glad you came."

Carley gave him a faint smile, "Same" she replied, still unsure if she was.

He grinned, "So did you enjoy the show?"

Carley instantly blushed. "I...I..., didn't mean to, it just happened to...I arrived at the wrong time... that's all," she said, trying hard to sound a little indignant.

He looked her straight in the eye and laughed. "I'm just teasing. At least now we're on an equal footing."

Her blush deepened as images of their lake encounter entered her mind. She stiffened, hating the fact that she always felt like a silly naive little schoolgirl around him. Why after all the men she had been with, was she having so much trouble with this one?

"Well I suppose to keep things respectable I had better go and get dressed" he said, handing her a cup of coffee as he brushed past her. Unprepared for her body's reaction to his touch, she found herself drawing in a quick sharp breath as a hot tingle shot across the surface of her skin. Her eyes followed him as he disappeared up the hall and into one of the rooms. Seeing a movement at the edge of the door frame nearly had her stepping to the side for a clearer view. She shook her head in disbelief, hadn't she already been caught spying once today? Why was the thing she wanted most something she could never have? Giving an exasperated sigh she turned her attention to the window. Why would he even want her? Look at him, he could have any woman he desired.

After a few minutes he came back up the hall wearing a pair of old faded jeans and a snug fitting white tee-shirt. She let out another little sigh; this was going to be a lot harder than she had ever imagined. Her thoughts were already heading in directions she didn't want them to, and she had only been in the room with him for a few minutes. Her eyes flicked to his. When he met her gaze she quickly turned away. He pointed to the couch. "Look why don't you take a seat?." He was a little worried, she had the look of someone who was about to flee. He should know; he had seen that look before. The thought of her watching him earlier had already aroused him and he couldn't stop thinking about it. His brow creased as he tried to focus. She looked so ill at ease. His heart clenched. Had he caused this? Giving him a weak smile she tried to get the images of his naked body out of her head. They both sat down, Dean chose to sit on the opposite couch, giving her a little space, not trusting himself to be that close to her. Since he had first laid eyes on her only days ago it was as if an invisible force was drawing him to her. Like a moth to a flame.

Her throat felt dry. She took a sip of her coffee, wishing he would stop staring at her that way. Her eyes met his over the rim of her cup "So you bought this place then."

"I did, though I have to say if it wasn't for my Uncle I would never have managed it. He was good enough to put up some of the finance," he gave a small laugh. "I think he got sick of me going on about it, but I couldn't let it go. I didn't want someone else owning it." He went quiet for a minute. "Sounds stupid I know, but..., well anyway I just had to have it."

Looking up she caught his eye and instantly knew why. He had fulfilled their dream from years ago. She shot to her feet, "Look, I'm sorry..., I don't think I can do this."

He quickly rose to meet her, reaching for her hand. Her eyes widened as his skin made contact with hers. She tried to draw her hand away but he held it firmly in his grasp. Her eyes dropped to the floor.

"Carley. Look at me."

Her head remained lowered as tears welled up behind her lashes. He took her chin lightly between his fingers and tilted her head up until she found herself staring into those beautiful green eyes. She blinked back her tears.

"Carley you can trust me. I haven't changed. I will always be here for you, no matter what."

Her lashes flicked across her damp eyes as she slowly shook her head side to side. "I'm not sure I can. I know I promised you an explanation, but it's not that easy... it's too... shameful."

Dean heart clenched as his eyes travelled her face; he could see the torment in her face. She looked so scared and vulnerable, just like the night she had run away from him. What if she ran again? His body tensed; he couldn't bear the thought of it. He released her chin and smiled at her reassuringly "How about we go and sit out beside the lake? We don't have to rush this if you're not ready." He squeezed her hand lightly. "Will you come and sit with me? Please?" Getting out of the confines of the room was just as much for his benefit as it was for hers. He was finding it increasingly difficult to be in the same room as her. They both needed a little a space. She nodded, thankful of the suggestion. It was taking all her self control not to fall into his arms. A small sigh escaped her lips, knowing that would be a huge mistake. She wasn't blind to the fact that the sexual tension between them was growing stronger by the minute. If she let her guard down for even for a second, there would be no turning back.

Still holding her hand he led her out to the lake edge. They slipped off their shoes and sat down, letting their legs dangle over the edge of the bank. A ritual they had performed so many times before. Only this time they made a point of sitting slightly apart ensuring their bodies didn't quite touch. She gazed out over the lake, thinking how lucky he was to wake up every morning to this. Shuffling forward she dipped her feet into the cool clear water, gliding them slowly back and forth as she watched the ripples rolling out across the surface of the lake. "It's so beautiful here" she said, watching her feet, still not trusting herself to look at him. She could feel his eyes on her.

"Yes it is," he replied, transfixed by her feet as they drifted silently through the water. Everything about her lately had his body in permanent state of arousal and having her sitting so close wasn't helping. "And so are you," he regretted it the moment he had said it.

Her feet stilled as she glanced up at him. "Beauty is only skin deep. You don't know me. I'm a different person to the one you once knew." She gave an exasperated sigh, "Will you please stop looking at me like that?"

He tensed. "Sorry" he replied, shifting to widen the gap between them and turning his attention towards the lake. They sat in silence, the tension between them slowly building. He stole a quick glance at her "This place was privately owned. I made it my mission to get the old man who lived here to sell it to me. I can tell you now it took quite a lot of persuading. I had to promise him that certain things wouldn't change." He paused, waiting for a response. When there wasn't one he decided to continue. "He used to watch us swimming from here. It was very overgrown then, which is probably why we never noticed the house sitting over here." That's why none of the local kids ever bothered with this place."

She turned to him. Of all the people in the world, if anyone were to understand it would be him. Clutching at that thought she tried to convince herself that it would all turn out for the best. He had stopped talking and was looking at her expectantly.

"Do you feel like talking? If not, I'm sure I could find something else to talk about until you are."

Her eyes were laced with uncertainty, "I'm ready." Her hands went to the hem of her skirt. Her fingers slowly moved back and forth along the seam.

"My.. my father... r...raped me," she blurted out. She heard his sharp intake of breath, but couldn't bring herself to look at him. It was too late to stop the words tumbling out of her mouth. "I was only fourteen. Tears pricked the back of her eyes. "I couldn't tell you, I..., I..., didn't want to risk... losing you."

He reached out for her, "Oh Carley."

Her hand shot up between them. "No please, let me finish."

Even though he had already heard enough, he nodded, understanding that she needed to get it out. Starting from that very first night her father had come stumbling into her room drunk, she slowly unravelled her sordid tale finally releasing all the secrets she had so carefully locked away. Dean remained stiff and silent, letting her pour her heart out. Even when the tears began to flow down her cheeks he refrained from touching her. He watched as the pain engulfed her. His chest tightened. After all these years he now knew why it was that she had left him. It was way beyond anything he had imagined. He had let her down and hadn't been there for her when she had needed him the most. It hurt to know that she had had to deal with the abuse alone. A lump formed in his throat as guilt settled over him. Why had he not seen her torment? He could have helped her and avoided all this pain. His back stiffened. How could he ever forgive himself for letting her down?

The door into her past now stood wide open. He now knew all the sordid details. She could sense him sitting next to her, his body stiff and rigid. He hadn't uttered a word since she had silenced him. Her hair fell down over her face as her head dropped forward in shame. Tears rolled down her cheeks and dripped into the water. Unable to bring herself to look at him, she stared vacantly down at her feet. If he rejected her now it would crush her heart into tiny little pieces. He was the only person who meant anything to her. Would he understand her pain? He reached out and gently brushed her hair back behind her shoulder.

"Carley, look at me."

Her head slowly shook from side to side as shame washed over her. He took her chin in his hand and turned her face up to his. She kept her eyes downcast, scared of what she might see.

"Carley?" he whispered quietly. Slowly her eyes turned up to his and she was surprised to see they were moist with tears. Deep lines creased his brow. He gave her a reassuring little smile as he gently brushed away her tears with his thumb. She let out a small gasp as he lent forward and placed a gentle kiss on her forehead. The tension she had felt earlier slowly began to ease. Her secret was finally out after all this time.

"It wasn't your fault. You know that don't you?"

She nodded. "You should have told me. I would have helped you" he said still holding her face in his hands, forcing her to look at him. Fresh tears began to trickle down her cheeks. He placed his arm around her shoulders drawing her against him. Her body stiffened. She wasn't ready for this. All she wanted to do was curl up in a ball and close out the outside world. Her head dropped down and settled against his chest. It was obvious that he wasn't repulsed by her. He had been there for her just as she hoped he would be . Now she wondered why she hadn't had the courage to tell him all those years ago when it could have made a difference. Why had she let herself be abused? Her tears trickled down her cheeks and onto his shirt, as she let herself be lulled by the simple sound of his strong rhythmic heartbeat. Slowly her body began relax. She let her weight rest against him. Her mind wandered back to a time she thought she had forgotten. Her hand came up to rest on his chest as she tried to absorb his strength. Everything felt so raw and painful, as if it had only happened yesterday. Was it just past emotions that had drawn them together? Her mind clouded; it felt surreal sitting there wrapped in his arms, the light brush of his lips on her forehead. Was it all just a dream? A small inkling of guilt sat in the back of her mind. She hadn't told him everything, she cringed inwardly. What would he think of her if he knew how she used to earn a living? It wasn't a risk she was willing to take. How could she possible live with losing him again? Not now, when she needed him so much. Deep down she already knew he would be repulsed. What man wouldn't be? With any luck she would never have to tell him. Who knew, after today they might simply go their separate ways. Or maybe they would just stay friends; not that she saw that as a possibility. Even now, after everything she had told him the sexual tension was still there. Up until now they had left it untouched, but something so strong didn't just simply go away.

He pulled her tighter against him knowing he would never forgive himself for missing the signs. It should have been obvious to him that something was wrong, but he had been too wrapped up with his own raging hormones to even notice. Guilt shot through him as he silently vowed to himself, that from now on he would protect her always. His jaw tightened. He still wasn't sure if she was going to stay and he wasn't about to ask her, not wanting to know the answer. Somehow he would have to convince her to stay. He didn't want to think of what life would be like without her. He already knew. Hadn't he waited long enough for her? He wasn't about to let her go again, not without a fight. He had failed her once and was determined he wasn't going to again. They would be good together. She may not realise it right now, but he would make her see. Fate had bought them together for a reason and the sooner she realised that the better it would be for both of them.

They stayed that way for a long time, wrapped in each other's arms. All the lost years seemed to fall away as he held her close. A feeling of numbness settled over her. She shivered as vivid memories of the abuse flared fresh in her mind. Over the years she had never really dealt with them, instead choosing to lock them away deep down inside. Now there was no hiding. How had she managed to survive? She knew the answer. By living a lie and pretending her life was something it wasn't. Guilt weighed down on her shoulders. In the beginning she could put it down to necessity. However as the years had passed, it was she who had chosen to stay in the city. Exhaustion finally crept up on her and her eyes began to close.

Dean nudged her, "Carley, come on inside, you need rest." She opened her eyes and nodded, not having the emotional strength to object. He slipped his arm from around her shoulders and got to his feet. She made no attempt to move. Her body now felt heavy and lifeless, as if it belonged to someone else. Crouching down beside her, he bent and scooped her up into his arms. He frowned, she felt so light, there was nothing to her. He carried her towards the house as she snuggled against his chest. He liked the feel of her in his arms. Walking through to his bedroom he laid her down on the bed, pulling the blankets up over her. He stood for a moment gazing down at her. She looked so peaceful; her face now showing no sign of the pain she had suffered. His lips brushed her forehead. A little murmur escaped her lips as she snuggled against the pillow. After drawing the blankets further around her, he moved to the door. Unable to resist he took one last glance back at her sleeping form, thankful that for now she was safe and under his care.

Chapter Fourteen

Carley woke to a chorus of bird song. The early morning sun was already stretching its warm rays out across the floor of the room. She stretched lazily as her eyes slowly adjusted to the light. Letting out a sudden gasp she sat up drawing the blankets around her. Memories of the previous day came flooding back. What had she told him? Everything? A small groan escaped her lips, how could she possible face him. Shame burned in the pit of her stomach. His masculine scent surrounded her as she drew the blanket up around her chin. With very little recollection of what had happened the day before she now wondered how he had taken the news. Her body stiffened. How did she even get into his bed? What if..., grabbing hold of the edge of the blankets she lifted them slowly and peered beneath. She gave a relieved sigh when she saw she was still fully clothed. Her head dropped back down onto the pillow. A deep frown appeared across her brow. What would he think of her now that he'd had time to digest what she had told him? Shoving back the blankets, she swung her legs over the side of the bed. She walked across to the window and pushed it open. The sun's early morning rays were just starting to touch the surface of the lake. Streams of light danced across the still water, making it shine like glass. Movement drew her eyes to the bank. She couldn't help smiling as she watched Dean pull food out of a bag and begin to throw it out to the various breeds of bird life. The grass quickly filled with hungry birds. As if sensing her there, he turned toward her. Their eyes locked momentarily. He gave her a wide generous smile. A quiver ran up her spine as she watched him turn back to his task. Drawing in a deep breath she slowly exhaled. He seemed fine, he... looked happy enough. She turned from the window and headed for the bathroom. Her eyes widened when she saw her reflection in the mirror. Red puffy eyes stared back at her, and her hair seemed to have discovered a mind of its own overnight. Wetting her hands under the tap she drew them over her hair forcing her fingers through the strands. After a few minutes she gave an exasperated sigh and gave up. It was the best she was going to be able to do under the circumstances. Splashing cold water on her face helped to make her feel more awake. She wet her finger and ran it around her teeth taking the time to study herself in the mirror. "Well Carley, this is it; make or break time." Turning from the mirror she headed outside. Her stomach tightened when she reached the front door. Taking a deep breath she stepped out into the sunlight and began to make her way towards him. She wouldn't gain anything by giving herself anymore time to think about it.

He gave her a warm smile as she approached him. "Good morning sleepy head. Did you have a good night?"

"Yes, thanks," she said glancing up at him.

He stood watching her. Her cheeks coloured. A smile touched his lips as he turned to throw out more food. "Glad to be of service."

She suddenly felt awkward and unsure what to do with her hands, finally choosing to cross them over her chest. As the minutes slowly ticked by, she began to become acutely aware of her closeness to him. Her eyes turned to the lake, but she could still sense his overwhelming presence closing in on her. There was a strong undercurrent moving between them and it slowly gaining momentum. Her body tensed, she couldn't let this happen; there were still too many secrets between them. It would be too easy to let him simply walk into her life. She glanced over at him. He was perfect. Handsome, charming, sexy and he genuinely cared about her. Her head slowly shook from side to side, it would be wrong, on so many levels.

His brow creased "Is something the matter?"

She looked down at her feet "No, I'm fine, I mean good."

His look intensified. "You don't look it. Come on Carley, what's bothering you?"

"It's just that..." her eyes moistened "I have to go, it's for the best."

"The best! I don't understand, the best for whom? It's certainly not for me."

She couldn't meet his eyes. Why was this so hard? Hadn't she already promised herself time to heal? She had to prove to herself that she could make it on her own. The real Carley was hidden deep inside her somewhere, and she intended to find her. No more pretending. Her eyes looked up at him pleadingly. "I need to do this, please don't make it any harder for me. Thank you for everything, but I really think it's best if I head back to the Motel."

Dean's stomach twisted, this is what he had feared. She was going leave. "Please Carley" he fought for something to say, anything to make her stay. "Won't you at least stay for breakfast? I'm cooking."

She didn't have the strength to resist him, not now, not ever. "In that case, definitely no thanks." She replied with a forced little laugh.

The hurt was clearly visible in his eyes. "I have to go now. Goodbye Dean, and thanks again."

He was trying hard not to look disappointed but there was no hiding it. Her teeth bit down on her bottom lip. Wasn't it better to let him down now, rather than later? Until she truly knew what it was she wanted, she couldn't be near him and risk hurting him all over again. Her eyes sought his. Maybe it was too late. Maybe she already had. Stifling a sob she turned and hurried up the drive, tears beginning to trickle down her cheeks.

Dean felt the same ache that he had felt twelve years ago when she had walked out of his life. "Carley wait."
She stopped and turned to look back at him.
He could see the tears. "Promise me one thing," he asked his voice catching in his throat. Her head slowly nodded. "If you do decide to leave, will you at least come and say goodbye?"
She stifled a loud sob. Why would he even have to ask? Of course she would. She gave a little sniff, "Sure..., I promise."
He nodded, unable to speak. Giving a short wave, she turned and continued up the drive, finally disappearing out of sight. Tears streamed down her cheeks, if she was doing the right thing, why did it hurt so damn much? Was she ever going to get anything right in her life? If only she knew how to put it right. She felt a tug on her heart as she thought about Dean. The look on his face had been so tragic, an ache lodged firmly in her heart. Could she really leave her past behind and move on?

Chapter Fifteen

Two weeks had gone by since she had last seen Dean, and she still seemed no closer to making a decision on what she wanted to do with her life. She had spent the last week furiously cleaning the house and had nearly finished it, all except for her old room which she still couldn't bring herself to enter. It was now Saturday morning and the thought of having to go back there yet again darkened her mood. All she wanted was to be finished with it. She hated the house with a growing vengeance. An unexpected knock came at her door. When she opened it she was surprised to see Nancy standing on the door step. "Good morning Carley. I'm sorry to bother you but I wondered if maybe you might like to come to dinner tonight?"

Carley stared at her blankly. "You've been working so hard on that house for weeks now. I thought you deserved a break. My husband's still away and I'm tired of eating alone. It would be just the two of us."

Carely tried not to appear shocked. She couldn't remember the last time she had been invited to dinner by anyone other than a paying client. "Ooh... um, yes that would be great..., um..., what time?"
Nancy smiled "How does six o'clock sound ?"
"I could be done by then..., thank you," replied Carley grinning widely.
Nancy turned to leave "Well, I'll see you about six then. You have a good day."
"I will," replied Carley. Well, there was a surprise. In the past few weeks she had slowly let Nancy peek into her life. It was nice to have someone to talk to, and Nancy seemed so accepting and non-judgemental. Carley was still smiling as she closed the door to her room and headed off towards the house. Her enthusiasm however wavered slightly as she turned into Edgewood Drive. Was she ever going to be able to rid herself of the damn house? Just the thought of it made her skin crawl.

It wasn't until she was almost at the gate that she saw him. Her body stiffened. She wasn't ready, not by a long shot. It had only been two weeks. Her heart rate began to accelerate. Here we go again, she thought to herself, as her body began to respond to him all on its own.
"Hi" he said casually, as if him sitting there was something she should be expecting.
He gave her one of his warm reassuring smiles causing her stomach to do a quick somersault. His eyes travelled up the long lean line of her exposed legs. He liked the way her tiny cut off shorts hugged the curve of her hips. He sucked in his breath at the sight of a strip of her flat tanned abdomen, teasing him from beneath her snug cropped top. His body tensed. He wasn't going to be able to keep this up much longer. He needed to convince her to stay and at least give them a chance

How did he manage to look so calm and collected all the time when she felt like a school girl with a crush? He wore a pair of faded jeans and a white fitted singlet. She gave a long swallow as her eyes skimmed across his thick muscular forearm that was resting across his raised knee. Her breath faltered. "Hi" she replied, "what are you doing here? I told you I needed more time."

He smiled, "I understand that, but I have my reasons. I called in on the off chance I might catch you here."

She stood her ground, not daring move any closer, "Dean, I can't do this, not now."

He held up his hand to silence her, "I'm not asking you to do anything. I respect your decision, honestly. But I felt today that you might make an exception."

She frowned as he held out a small white cardboard box. "Happy Birthday"

Her mouth dropped open. "Ooh! What? No, it can't be." How could she have forgotten her own birthday? Her hand flew to her mouth. "So it is." She gave a little laugh." I can't believe I forgot my own birthday. With everything that's been going on, it completely slipped my mind." Carley looked at the box that he held out for her. As she stepped forward to take it from him, she instantly became aware of the magnitude of his maleness. She had been pushing herself hard for the past week so as not to give herself any time to think about him. A lot of good that had done her; she was now right back where she had started. Tentatively she reached out and took the box from him, being careful not to let her skin touch his. She glanced down at him shyly. "Thanks," she whispered.

He smiled. "My pleasure, now open it."

She carefully drew open the flap and let out a delighted gasp. Tears instantly sprang to her eyes. A small chocolate cupcake sat in the centre of the box, adorned with a coating of pink icing and a single candle pushed in the centre.

His eyes met hers "You don't have to worry, I'm not going to break into song,"

She laughed for the first time in weeks "I'm glad to hear it. I'm not sure my nerves could handle it. I don't know what to say. This is the best present ever" Without thinking she bent down and gently kissed him on the cheek. With a sudden gasp she pulled back, unprepared for the quick flare of heat that had shot through her body. Her eyes met his. She could almost hear the sexual tension sizzling between them. He reached out and took a firm grip of her arm. A surprised yelp escaped her lips as she was pulled down into his lap. The box slid from her hand and landed on the step next to them.

She struggled, pushing her hand against him, trying to free herself from his grasp. "The cake."

He wasn't about to give in that easily; he glanced down at the box "The cake's fine, see?"

He was right. Sure enough it was sitting safely on the step beside them. Placing her hand against his chest she pushed against him, "Dean I can't do this, please let me go."

He held her tightly with no intention of letting her go; finally her body stilled. She daren't take a breath. Wasn't this where she had dreamed of being, wrapped in his strong muscular arms? His warm breath brushed against the side of her neck causing her body to quiver. Her heart rate quickened. She could feel his muscular chest pressing up against her body and his strong solid thighs beneath her easily supporting her weight. Defeated, she slumped against him. What was the point of fighting it?

He relaxed his grip a little. "Now that's more like it."

She felt a strange type of comfort being wrapped in his arms. He had always been her protector. He didn't have anything to prove to her. She knew in her heart she could trust him with her life. Her head dropped against his shoulder. She didn't have the willpower to fight against the feelings now welling up inside her. Since that first day they had met, it seemed as though they had both been locked into some sort of mating ritual. Her nerve endings felt raw and inflamed. A soft moan eased out through her lips as he laid gentle kisses at the base of her neck. He felt her quiver. Her eyes sought his. The intensity in them scared her a little. He gently placed his lips on hers, kissing her softly, savouring the taste of her. A small low growl vibrated through his chest causing her nipples to peak and her insides to clench. Now unable to control his deep unrelenting desire for her, he pressed down harder, capturing her lips with his. She responded willingly with equal intensity, as they gave into the powerful forces they had been fighting against for weeks. Heat flared between them unleashing the passion they had tried so hard to disguise. His mouth pressed firmly down onto hers as he feverously devoured her soft full lips. Her lips parted. His tongue slowly travelled along the inside of her lip. Again he felt her quiver. He dove in deeper their tongues now entwined in a passionate dance. He could feel the erratic beat of her heart as her body yielded to his. He clung to her tightly, expecting that at any moment she would leap from his arms and flee. Little did he know that she too was trapped by the intensity of her need. She could feel his strong powerful heartbeat racing beneath her and knew that she alone had the ability to do this to him, as he did to her. Her hand glided over the taut muscles of his chest and she was rewarded with a deep groan. Her body trembled as his slightly roughened hands met with the smooth skin on her back. She faltered for a second, frightened by the depth of her feelings for him. A hungry urgency began to grow deep down inside her. A gentle pulsing now emanated from her very core. As she shifted on his lap he quickly gripped her hips, stilling her. His strong erection pressed against the back of her thighs. Her eyes widened as she realized there had been no feeling of revulsion. Something she had grown so accustomed to expecting over the years. She pushed against his chest trying to free herself. Had he unknowingly broken through her barriers? She was now totally exposed and vulnerable. What was she doing? She had let down her defences and left herself wide open for more hurt and heartache. Her mind went wild with panic. This hadn't been the plan. Her body went rigid, "Let me go."

He tightened his grip; he wasn't going to let her run, not this time. His brow creased. Something was holding her back, but what? She tried to get to her feet but his arm was still firmly looped around her waist. Defeated she fell back down onto his lap. Hadn't he been patient long enough? Couldn't she see that they were meant to be together? He wasn't one to give up so easily. She dared a glance at him, instantly knowing it had been a mistake. A quick sear of heat flared up inside her. His jaw tightened "You want to be here. I can see it in your eyes. So why are you fighting it?"

Her eyes moistened. She couldn't risk hurting him, not again. Did she even know what love was? He deserved to be loved unconditionally. Was she even capable of that?

"Dean, I've already told you. I needed more time."

He looked into her eyes, "I know..., and I'm willing to give you as much time as you need..., within reason."

"So why do this?"

He gave her a sheepish smile, "I thought maybe you needed a little taste of what you're missing."

As much as she tried, she couldn't help letting a slight smile touch the corner of her lips. "Oh, don't you worry, I'm fully aware of what I'm missing."

His brow creased, "So why the hesitation?"

She shook her head slowly from side to side. "Dean, I thought you of all people would understand. I've hurt you once already. I couldn't live with myself if I hurt you all over again. I still don't know why you forgave me in the first place.

"Carley, don't you think that's up to me? Surely you can't believe you are to blame. If you're going to blame anyone it should your father and possibly me."

Her head snapped around. "You? How could you possibly be to

blame?"

"It's simple. I wasn't there for you when you needed me. I didn't see that you were hurting. All I was thinking about was getting into your pants."

Carley laughed, "So nothing much has changed then."

He smiled "I guess not. But at least I'm being honest."

Her heart clenched. At least someone was. She turned to look at him. Could she risk telling him everything? Her shoulders slumped. No she couldn't. There was something between them, that was plainly obvious but she couldn't let it go any further. Dean brushed his hand lightly across her cheek. Her body quivered.

"Look Carley I don't need you to worry about me. I already know what I want. Life is all about risks, and unless you are willing to take them you will never know if it was the right thing or not. There is no sure thing, not even for us."

She sat silently, looking down at her hands, fully aware of what her body wanted but as for her heart, she was still unsure. It had been locked away for so long now, she wasn't even sure if she knew what love was. "Dean, there are things you don't know about me."

He placed his fingers on her chin and turned her head so she had no option but to look at him. "I don't care about the past. It's now I'm interested in."

"But you don't understand, I..."

"Carley honestly, it's fine. There is time for all that later. I'm not asking for any promises. All I want is for you to take a risk and see where it leads." He sat there hoping for a response, but when there was none forthcoming he pushed a little harder. He needed to break through to her.

"Come out to my place."

Her eyes widened.

A smile touched his lips, "To talk; we need to see if we can make this work."

She hesitated. Hadn't she promised herself more time? Looking at him now, she resigned herself to the fact that time wouldn't change a thing. If twelve years apart hadn't killed the flame, then no amount of stalling would either. With an exasperated sigh she nodded "Fine, but no lap sitting, or kissing... You have to promise."

He gave her a wickedly charming smile "I promise." He said as he pushed her off his knee. She let out a little yelp as she hit the grass with a thud. She got to her feet rubbing her backside. Her eyes narrowed, "What the hell did you go and do that for?"

He grinned, "A promise is a promise. No lap sitting allowed." She threw her head back and laughed until tears trickled down her cheeks. "I will get you back for that, you know I will."

He grinned. "I look forward to it."

Her eyes shone at the challenge. Dean got up off the step and she suddenly felt small against his broad muscular frame. He made a move to leave. "I had better get going. I'm supposed to be at work. I will see you tomorrow, about noon." He didn't wait for an answer as he placed his hands either side of her face and tilted her head back so she again found herself staring into his deep green eyes. His thumb gently brushed across her lips. "Remember I'm not looking for any promises. Just give us a chance to get to know each other again. That's all I ask."

She watched him go, wondering why she always felt so out of control whenever he was around. Her fingers toyed with the bracelet on her wrist. Taking it off now would be like breaking an unwritten bond. He disappeared from sight. She turned and climbed the steps. It wasn't until she reached the kitchen that she remembered the cake. Letting out a gasp she rushed back outside and scooped it up off the step. Once inside she placed it down on the kitchen counter and flipped the lid open. It was hard to believe that he had remembered... after all this time. Reaching in she carefully lifted the cake out of the box and took a bite. "Mmm..." Chocolate, her favourite. Happy Birthday Carley" she said between giggles. How could she have forgotten her own birthday "Twenty seven years old today?" It only seemed like yesterday that she and Dean were children sitting out at the lake front. Dean's present had easily out shone the red Porsche she had received for her last birthday. And the kiss couldn't have been more perfect..., for their first kiss. Maybe he was right. It was about time she stopped over thinking everything. She couldn't help wondering if she should have come clean about her past. But telling him she had been a prostitute wasn't something you just blurted out and wouldn't be something he would accept lightly. Anyway, hadn't he said it could wait? She licked her fingers clean. If she really deserved a chance at happiness, why did she feel so damn guilty? Scraping the last of the crumbs from the box she let out a long sigh. Her life was never going to be easy. Placing the box in the trash can she scooped up the cleaning equipment and headed upstairs.

Glancing at the clock, she was surprised to see how quickly the time passed. It was already four thirty. If she didn't hurry she would be late for dinner. She put all her cleaning equipment away and walked out, locking the door behind her. Her mind wandered to the day ahead. Where would it lead? How much longer could she fight against the strong attraction she felt toward him?

Chapter Sixteen

She arrived back at the Hotel with only just enough time to get cleaned up and make it to Nancy's front door by six o'clock. Her shoulders were tense as she knocked on the door. After what seemed like an eternity it opened.

"Hello dear, come on in" Nancy said gesturing for Carley to enter and closing the door behind them. "I so glad you could come. So tell me, how was your day?"

Carley smiled, as thoughts of the kiss entered her mind, "I had a great day and got quite a lot done on the house." Her eyes travelled the room, "I've nearly finished. It should be ready for painting by the end of the month." Nancy's house was warm and cosy. It reminded her of her mother. It wasn't often that she felt the loss of her mother but standing here in the middle of Nancy's lounge caused a sudden sense of loneliness to close in around her.

"Dinner shouldn't be long. Why don't you have a seat while I go and finish up in the kitchen?"

Carley sat down on the sofa by the window. She could hear Nancy moving around in the kitchen. A feeling of emptiness began to well up inside her. Getting to her feet she walked into the kitchen. Nancy was standing at the stove, her back turned. Carley's chest suddenly tightened, as childhood visions of her mother flooded back. The colour drained from her face. Nancy turned and instantly dropped what she was doing to rush to Carley's side.

"What's the matter dear? Here, you had better sit down," she said dragging over a chair.

Carley gratefully dropped into it, the colour now slowly returning to her cheeks.

Nancy continued to fuss around her, "Would you like a coffee or a glass of water? You gave me quite a scare."

Carley looked up at her and smiled weakly, "I'm fine, really, maybe I overdid it at the house today. I haven't really been eating all that well lately. I think it's all catching up on me."

Nancy wasn't convinced, but she didn't push it. Filling a glass of water, she placed it on the table in front of Carley.

Carley looked up apologetically "I'm sorry. I don't mean to be a bother."

Nancy patted her hand "Nonsense dear, don't even give it another thought. We all need someone to lean on from time to time. It's nothing to be ashamed of. Do you think maybe you took on a little bit much with the house?"

Carley stared down at her glass. "Maybe I did," she hesitated "You reminded me of my mother. She passed away when I was young. When I saw you standing over there I thought..., I miss her sometimes." A single tear rolled down her cheek.

Nancy stepped over and wrapped her arms around her shoulders. Carley's body went rigid then slowly relaxed as tears began to flood down her cheeks. She hadn't cried for her mother for quite some time and it felt good to let it all out.

When the sobbing eased, Nancy slipped her arms from around her "We all need a good cry occasionally. It does us good."

Carley looked up, noticing Nancy's eyes also appeared a little glassy. She smiled "You know, I think you're right. I certainly needed that." Nancy brushed her hand across her shoulder "As I said before, lovey, my door is always open. If ever you need someone to talk to I'm always here." Not wanting to smother the poor girl she turned her attention back to the kitchen and before long she was placing a huge roast meal on the table. Carley hadn't realised how hungry she was until she saw the food and her mouth began to water. There hadn't been a good home cooked meal placed in front of her since... A lump caught in her throat, her mother last cooked her one. Carley swallowed back more tears "Thank you. It all looks wonderful."

Nancy smiled "You're welcome, any time you feel like a home cooked meal you need only ask."

They ate their meal in silence Carley enjoying every mouthful. When she had finished she placed her knife and fork down on her plate and sighed. "I can easily say that's the best meal I've had in years. Nothing beats a good home cooked meal."

Nancy smiled "Thank you, that's so sweet."

With the meal finished they began chatting. It started with the house. Then Nancy moved on, and spoke a little of her husband Robert, whom Carley was yet to meet. Carley finally found herself talking about Dean. She told Nancy about the cupcake and how she had forgotten it was her birthday. The kiss she left as her little secret. As the evening wore on Carley found herself relaxing. Her guard began to slip away. There was one question however, that she had been dying to ask all evening. "Nancy..."

"Yes dear."

"How did you know Robert was the right one? How did you know you were in love?"

Nancy's chest tightened but she smiled reassuringly, "I assume we are talking about Dean?."

Carley stiffened. She should have guessed Nancy would see right through her. Colour rose to her cheeks "How did you know?"

Nancy face softened "You have mentioned him quite a few times tonight."

Carley's fingers toyed with the stitching on the sofa.

Nancy gave a little chuckle. "Let's see. Tell me how you feel about him."

Carley squirmed in her seat "That's the thing. I'm not sure. All I know is that I turn into a blithering idiot whenever he's near. I miss him when he's not around and I can't stop thinking about him."

Nancy sat quietly for a minute.

Carley looked up at her "And he makes me laugh and my heart races whenever I'm near him."

Nancy gave a deep hearty laugh "Oh my, I hate to be the one to tell you, but you've got it bad."

Carley frowned "Bad? I don't understand."

Nancy smiled, "I'd say by what you have just told me that you have definitely found the right one. So, how does he feel about you?" She thought back to the kiss and the present he had bought her that morning, "I'm pretty sure he feels the same way." A frown crept across her brow, "I don't want to hurt him. What if I'm not capable of loving him?"

Nancy leant over and took Carley's hands in her own. How could such a beautiful young woman feel so incapable of love? What had this poor girl been through? "Look Carley, even after what you have told me, nothing is for certain in love or life but if you don't give love a chance you will never know if he is the right one or not. Just let your heart guide you and stop worrying about the final outcome. Take it one step

at a time. You never know, you might enjoy the ride."
Carley smiled. There was no doubt in her mind about that. She had thought of little else over the past couple weeks. "Maybe you're right. Dean said very much the same thing to me this morning. I think you'd like him.
Nancy patted her hand "He sounds wonderful, I'm sure I would."
"He's invited me out to his place tomorrow."
Nancy raised her eyebrows, "I hope you're going."
Carley smiled "I am, but just to talk."
Nancy nodded and didn't say a word.
"Nancy. Thank you for listening, and for all your advice. I feel a lot better about things since talking to you."

As the night wore on Carley opened up to Nancy more. She relayed the whole sordid story about the abuse she had suffered at her father's hands. Nancy was shocked to say the least and found it rather hard to listen to. However she was pleased to hear that Carley had already told Dean, and that he had been very understanding and supportive. She now saw Carley a little differently, realizing how hard it must have been for her to go to her father's funeral and enter that house. Nancy admired the way Carley was trying to put her past behind her and get her life back on track. It was obvious she was a fighter, and Nancy felt privileged to have been included in her life.

Finally at nearly midnight, the evening drew to a close. Carley stretched and rose to her feet. Nancy walked her to the door. Carley turned and hugged her.
"Thank you again for a lovely meal and for listening. It means a lot." She leaned in and kissed Nancy on the cheek "Goodnight."
"Goodnight lovey" Nancy called as she watched her cross the parking lot. "There goes one very brave woman", thought Nancy to herself. She stood at the door watching until Carley was safely in her room. When

she saw the light go on, Nancy closed the door.

Carley stripped out of her clothes and threw herself down on the bed. She smiled. It had been a lot easier telling her story for the second time. Maybe now she could finally stop running from her past and look toward the future.

Chapter Seventeen

Carley slept late for the first time since she had been back. When she finally woke she glanced over at the clock. Throwing the covers back she got to her feet and gave her body a long stretch. Today was the start of something new; she could feel it deep down in the pit of her stomach. Life could only get better from here, she was sure of it. She walked into the bathroom.

Freshly showered she made her way over to the closet. Today called for something a little more feminine. She slipped her short white layered skirt off the hanger. It had always managed to draw a little attention. Pulling it up her legs she fastened it, tugging it down so it sat low on her hips. A satisfied smile creased her lips as she gave a little twirl in front of the mirror. Selecting her dark blue waistcoat from the drawer, she held it up in front of her. She put it on ensuring to leave the top button undone. Tipping her head forward, she brushed her hair out then flicked her head back, letting it fall softly around her shoulders. Her reflection smiled back at her. He had always liked it when she wore her hair out. Wiggling into a pair of skimpy white lace underwear she considered herself almost ready to go. She slipped on a pair of leather sandals. With one last look in the mirror she gave a satisfied smile and turned away.

Slinging her handbag across her shoulder, she snatched her sunglasses from the counter and headed out the door. Nancy walked towards her from across the parking lot

"Good morning Carley, I wanted to wish you luck," she winked "For today, not that I think you will need it wearing that," she said with a twinkle in her eye.

Carley's cheeks flushed, "Umm, thanks, I think."

Nancy laughed, waving her on "Go, enjoy."

Carley smiled "I will, and thanks again." With that she headed off up the drive, humming to herself. As she turned onto the main street she was again struck by how little it had changed. She smiled, but honestly she wouldn't want to change a thing. It was nice not to feel the pressures of a big city weighing down on her shoulders. Here everyone seemed relaxed and simply strolled along without feeling the need to rush. People all greeted each other by their first names; except her of course. It hurt to know that the town didn't want her here and that she no longer belonged. So she had disappeared into the night. Surely she wasn't the first child to run away from home? She let out a startled gasp at the sound of a loud wolf whistle. Her head spun around. Spider was hanging out of the window of a bright red sports car. He drew up beside her, matching her pace, a sloppy grin plastered on his face.

"Hey! Carl's, you're looking mighty fine today. You want a lift?."

She smiled "Thanks, but no thanks, I'm enjoying the walk."

Several people on the street had turned to look.

He patted the seat beside him, "Come on, you know you want to."

Her eyes narrowed "I said no."

"Oh, come on, I won't bite."

"I'm not willing to risk it. I haven't had my shots."

He grinned. "A little feisty today I see, I like that in a woman."

She drew to a stop, crossing the road behind the car to the other side of the street. He leaned out the window "It's your loss baby." he yelled, as he hit the gas and disappeared in a squeal of tyres up the main street. Crossing back over she turned into the side street, suddenly gratefully to be off the main road. Spider was certainly persistent. Her brow creased, almost too persistent.

Dean paced the lawn. He hadn't been able to sleep and had found himself out at the lake edge watching the sunrise. Since daybreak he had been running around madly getting everything ready. Now that it was, he couldn't seem to settle. For the twentieth time he glanced at his watch. What if she decided not to come? He glanced at his watch again; it was one minute past twelve. Maybe she was running late. He groaned as he paced back and forth. He glanced up and spotted her through the trees. Relief washed over him. A wide smile broke out across his face. She was smiling too. Surely that was a good sign. He stood rooted to the spot as he watched her round the bend and make her way towards him. His breath caught in this throat as he watched her short skirt sway back and forth across her tanned thighs. He let out a soft groan as his eyes travelled up the length of her body, taking in all her womanly curves. Her snug fitting waist coat finished just above her navel, giving him a good glimpse of the tempting slice of tanned flesh just above the waist band of her skirt.

He felt himself harden. Her hair was loose; as she walked it bounced lightly around her shoulders. Had she worn it that way for his benefit?

She drew to a stop in front of him. "By the look of that silly grin, I take it you're glad to see me," she said giving a nervous little laugh. His body tensed, "I was starting to think you wouldn't show."

She moved closer, locking eyes with him "I'm not in the habit of going back on my word."

He grinned. "Is that right? Well I'll be sure to remember that." Her face heated at the intensity of his stare. Was she going to be able to pull this off? Could she prolong the inevitable? She could already feel the sexual energy sizzling between them. Her heart rate quickened. Struggling to keep her emotions in check, she gave him what she hoped was a confident smile. Her breath was suddenly forced out of her lungs when he grabbed her around the waist and drew her against him. He held her there, breathing in the soft scent of jasmine on her skin. She didn't struggle this time. His eyes sought hers their intensity leaving no doubt in her mind what it was he wanted. She gave a teasing smile. She wasn't about to make it easy for him "Didn't you promised to behave?."

He gave a low growl and reluctantly released her.

Her eyelashes fluttered "So what's for lunch. I'm absolutely starving."

He smiled. "I know what I'd like to have for lunch."

Her tongue slowly moved across her lips. "Hmmm... is that right? Well I'm sorry to be the one to tell you, but that's not on the menu." His eyes darkened, "Is that right? Well I might just have to see what I can do about that...," he grabbed her hand. "But right now, we eat." He led her over towards the lake and stopped in front of a table and chairs he had positioned beside the water's edge. He grinned inwardly. Before this day was over he would possess her mind, body and soul, and she would beg for him to break his promise. He pulled out the chair "Your seat madam." He helped her to get seated "Would madam care for some refreshments, wine perhaps" he asked trying to keep a straight face as he put on a posh English accent.

She smiled "Why yes, that would be absolutely lovely, thank you" she replied, playing along.

"I'll be back in a jiffy Madam" he turned and headed towards the house and soon returned with a bottle of expensive looking wine and two glasses. He placed them on the table, then headed back into the house, returning with a tray piled high with an array of tantalising morsels.

She clapped her hands playfully "Oh... I feel so spoilt."

He had gone to so much trouble. The tray was filled with an assortment of crackers and cheeses, club sandwiches which had been placed around a large bunch of black grapes.

She glanced over at him and smiled "It looks great, but you didn't have to go to so much trouble. Sandwiches and a Coke would have sufficed." She picked up a piece of cheese and popped it into her mouth, "I'm easily pleased," she purred seductively.

His eyebrows shot up. He grinned, taking a bow "As always, I'm at your service."

Her eyes brightened "Always huh?" she picked up a grape and sucked it slowly into her mouth.

He tensed as his eyes sought hers. A small quiver ran up her spine. He slipped into the seat opposite her; she seemed different today. More like the Carley he had grown to love. His hopes rose. Maybe now that she had told him about her father, she would see that there was no reason for them not to be together.

They quickly demolished all the food on the tray and over three quarters of the bottle of wine.

She let out a little giggle "I think I had better go easy on the wine. I'm already starting to feel a little tipsy. I guess that's what happens when you don't eat breakfast."

Dean made a mental note, not to bring out the other bottle of wine. The last thing he wanted was her drunk. He stood up, picking up the empty tray, "I'll be back in a minute."

Carley leaned back in her chair "Take your time. I'm not going anywhere."

He smiled "Glad to hear it'" he turned and headed towards the house. She gasped, her eyes widening when he appeared carrying a small plate with a large piece of boysenberry cheesecake on it.

"No way, this is beyond amazing" She glanced up at him and smiled "And totally unexpected.

You sure know how to show a girl a good time, don't you?"

His eyes met hers and she felt the colour rise to her cheeks.

"I don't remember you ever blushing."

Her eyes narrowed "I'm not," her blush deepened, she gave a sigh "Okay so I'm blushing."

He smiled "I like it."

She broke off a forkful of cheesecake and offered it to him. He opened his mouth and let her put it in. She smiled and broke off a piece for herself. In a few minutes, the plate was empty.

"That was delicious." Her fingers wiped across the plate gathering the last of the crumbs. She sucked her fingers and he felt himself harden. She glanced up at him and smiled.

If he moved too fast, he could run the risk of losing her for good. He held out his hand, she smiled placing hers in his.

"How about we go and sit by the lake?"

"Sounds great," she said, her eyes holding a look of uncertainty. She followed him to the water's edge. Slipping off her sandals she sat down, dipping her feet into the water. He sat down beside her and placed his feet in the water alongside hers. Turning her face up to the sun she closed her eyes and drew in a deep breath. When she opened them again she was surprised to see that he had already stripped off his shirt. Her stomach clenched at the sight of his toned chest and abdomen. He flopped back down on the grass, and closed his eyes. As the minutes ticked by, she became acutely aware of the warmth of his thigh pressing up against hers. She glanced over her shoulder at him. How was it he always looked so at ease? Her eyes travelled the lines of his body. He lay on his back with his fingers locked behind his head. His large biceps bulged. She watch his chest rise and fall as he breathed. How was it that he could be so relaxed when her nerves where all shot to hell? Her eyes travelled the length of his body, hovering for a second over the sizeable mound in his shorts. Her heart rate increased as she imagined what it would be like to run her hands over his body. Her body hummed with anticipation. She flipped over onto her stomach and rested her chin on her hands so she could look at him. Her fingers brushed lightly down the side of his body. He drew in a sharp breath but didn't move or open his eyes. Feeling bolder she traced a line around the outside edge of his nipple. He raised his head and looked at her with one eye still closed "I'd be careful if I was you. There is only so much teasing a man can take."

She smiled as she playfully pinched his nipple.

He dropped his head back down onto his hands "don't say I didn't warn you."

She moved in beside him, memorized by the rhythmic rise and fall of his chest. His breathing she noticed was now a little deeper. Her fingertips brushed across his abdomen just above the waistband on his shorts. She felt him draw in a deep breath. Smiling she reached up and placed a soft kiss in the middle of his chest. His body went tense as her hair trailed across his skin. His lips twitched. Her brow creased. He was playing with her. The thought only made her more determined. He was going to break his promise one way or another. The moment she had left the motel, her mind had been made up and she wasn't about to back out now. She slowly trailed her hands down over his solid thighs. His body tensed under her touch but still he did nothing. On her arrival she had had him figured as a sure bet. Now she wasn't so sure.

Frustrated, she got to her feet. She had come this far and she was determined that she was not going to take no for an answer.

He opened one eye and looked up at her. "Are you going somewhere?"
"Maybe" she replied, giving him a seductive little smile. If this didn't
push him over the edge and show him she meant business then nothing
would. As she moved along the bank she slowly began to unfasten her
waist coat. He drew himself up into a sitting position. She smiled to
herself, secure in the knowledge that she now had his full attention.
There was a sharp intake of breath as she let her waistcoat drop to the
ground. Her upper body was now completely exposed. Her nipples
peaked. If there was one thing she had learnt it was the art of teasing.
She reached up and drew her hands through her hair, tossing it onto her
back. Dean slowly rose to his feet as she pulled down the zip on her
skirt eased it down over her hips. It dropped to her feet. Flicking it to
the side with her foot, she turned and gave him a teasing little smile.
Her fingers moved to her pretty lace underwear. She rolled them down
her legs and stepped out of them. He let out a deep groan. The sunlight
glistened along the smooth planes of her body. She drew up onto her
toes raising her arms above her head. He stood riveted to the spot, his
heart now thumping wildly in his chest. His strong erection strained
against the front of his shorts. It was as if the past few weeks had been
one long tantalising act of foreplay leading them to this precise moment
in time. He let out a low growl and moved towards her. She grinned and
sprang from the bank, disappearing below the surface of the water. He
was still standing on the bank when she resurfaced a few feet from
shore.
"So, are you coming in, or what?"
He didn't need to be asked twice as he quickly stripped off his shorts.
She laughed as she watched him struggling out of his clothing as fast as
humanly possible. He headed for the bank. Carley quivered as her eyes
raked across his naked body. She could see he was already highly
aroused. Her heart rate quickened, there certainly wouldn't be any
turning back now. Did she love him? She still wasn't sure. The one
thing she did know was that she wanted him now more than anything

else she had ever wanted in her life. All her earlier reservations had simply evaporated the moment she had entered the water. She was finally exactly where she wanted to be. A small quiver ran the length of her body knowing he had the ability to take her places she had never before been. When she was younger she hadn't wanted, nor had she known how to handle his advances. She smiled. Now was a whole different story. If there was one thing that all this had taught her, it was that a good man was hard to find. Her stomach clenched as she looked up at him. She was pretty sure she had found hers. Just maybe, if she was lucky enough, she might get her' happily ever after' she had always dreamed of.

He dove off the bank, entering the water in an untidy splash, causing a large wave to wash across the surface of the lake towards her. A little voice in the back of her head kept telling her that she was deceiving him. That she should tell him about all the men she had been with. But how could she? He was the best thing that had ever happened to her. Why would she want to throw it all away, over a past she couldn't change? Finally she had a chance to live a new life. Didn't she a least deserve that? The surface of the lake remained empty she glanced around; he hadn't yet resurfaced. She let out a sudden gasp as his hands closed around her waist. He lifted her out of the water and tossed her backwards. She hit the water with a loud ungainly splash and disappeared below the surface. She resurfaced shoving her wet hair back off her face. Her eyes narrowed.

He grinned, "Bring back any fond memories?"

A smile creased her lips as she swiped her arm across the surface dousing him full in the face with water. He shook his head, a challenging glint appearing in his eye.

"You do know that's going to cost you, don't you?"

Giving a loud squeal she turned away from him and began swimming like she'd never swum before. Even though she already knew that the chances of getting away from him were almost zero to none. Dean watched as she fought to put some distance between them. His urgency growing stronger with every stroke she took. He still couldn't believe she had actually come back. He had given up on the hope of ever seeing her again. It had been difficult for him to sit there and listen to her telling him about her father and what he had done to her, right under his nose. He was determined to erase all those bad memories and replace them with good ones. No, amazing ones. The tension began to build. He felt like a wild animal ready to strike. A hungry urgency was now growing deep down inside him. She had put quite a distance between them and he couldn't bring himself to wait any longer. He dove below the surface and when he finally re-surfaced he had already gained some distance. His anticipation began to grow with every powerful stoke of his arms, drawing him ever closer.

She could hear him now. Frantically she tried to swim faster. Her heart began to beat wildly in her chest. Pure adrenalin coursed through her veins. A part of her wanted to be caught but the other was still a little unsure. As much as she tried to push aside her insecurities, they still played in the forefront of her mind. Was it because now she had something to lose? She let out an ear piercing scream as his hand wrapped around her ankle and she felt herself being pulled backwards through the water. He gathered her up into his arms trapping her against his body. As if by instinct she began to struggle. He pulled her tighter against his chest, kicking frantically as he tried to keep them both above water line. He had waited twelve long years to have her in his arms he wasn't about to let her get away this time.

She stilled, unsure of why she had been struggling in the first place. Her body went limp as she looked up at him. His need was evident as he drew her closer. Her body stiffened, then just as quickly she melted against him. His taut muscles held her tightly against his chest. Her eyes widened slightly as she felt his strong erection pressing against her lower abdomen. Her pulse quicken as an unexpected moan escaped her lips. He smiled, lightly brushing his lips against hers. He hesitated, needing some reassurance from her. Her tongue lightly licked across his lower lip. The fire she had ignited inside him only days before suddenly turned into a raging inferno heating him through to his core. Placing his lips firmly down on hers he devoured them in a hungry frenzy. When he finally released them they were pink and swollen. He tailed soft kisses along her jaw line and down the long slender line of her neck, causing every nerve in her body to tingle. As they lost themselves in each other, they would dip below the water's surface, only to resurface and begin all over again. He suddenly drew back, his eyes searching hers. He needed to know for sure if she was ready and that he wasn't moving too fast. She looked back at him her eyes now deep blue pools of smouldering shameless longing. Giving an impatient groan, he eased her away. Taking a firm grip of her wrist he began to tow her to shore. Their progress was slow, as they stopped at regular intervals to get another taste of what lay ahead. Her body quivered with anticipation. In the past she had always been the one in control. It was something she always felt she needed. She smiled. Now she knew it was way more exciting to let someone else take control. Her body relaxed as she let herself be drawn to shore.

Chapter Eighteen

A quick pang of guilt shot through her as they approached the lake edge. Didn't he deserve to know what kind of woman he was getting involved with? She knew without a doubt that telling him would ruin everything. What man would want to know that the woman they were about to make love to had been with so many other men and been paid for it. Her heart clenched; even though she hated the thought of lying to him she knew she couldn't tell him. Didn't she deserve a little happiness in her life? After everything she had been through, why could she not have the one thing she wanted more than anything else?

They reached the bank. Dean climbed out. She smiled as she watched his muscular thighs flex as he heaved himself up onto the bank. He turned, offering her his hand. She hesitated. He was so magnificent. Way too good for the likes of her. Reaching up she placed her hand in his. He pulled her up onto the bank beside him. She flopped down onto the grass unsure if her legs would actually hold her. As much as she was used to being naked she found it a little unnerving, now there was nothing for her to hide behind. This was real, with no more pretence. He dropped down beside her and turned to face her. She looked at him through lowered lashes. He smiled, brushing a lock of her hair back behind her shoulder. His eyes told her everything she needed to know. She could still see the carefree young boy she had grown to trust..., and love. Her body quivered, only now he was a man who still wanted her, after everything she had put him through. It all felt surreal, like a dream that she would suddenly awaken from.

He brushed his thumb lightly across her lips. A single tear trickled from the corner of her eye and rolled down her cheek. He brushed it away tenderly. A deep crease appeared on his brow.

"Are you sure you want this?" he asked softly.

She nodded, smiling hesitantly. He leant over and kissed her lightly on the lips then drew back, his eyes searching hers. The urge to have her was getting stronger by the minute but he had to be sure she was ready. He trailed his fingers lightly along her collar bone and down between her breasts. She tipped her head back, pushing her breast forward. His fingers brushed across her nipple and it peaked instantly. He gently rolled it between his thumb and forefinger. She let out a soft moan, arching her back, offering herself to him. He lowered his lips, sucking her nipple into his mouth, teasing its hardened tip with his tongue. A small whimper escaped her lips as he released the first and gave the second the same attention. He was determined to take his time and savour every tantalising inch of her.

The intensity of his touch sent heat coursing though out her body. Doubt began to creep in. Did she dare give herself to someone so completely and let go of all restraint? He released her nipple and trailed his hand across her stomach and down over her abdomen. Her already sensitive skin flared with heat as he moved his hand in slow tantalizing circles. She drew in a sharp breath as his fingers reached the small narrow strip of neatly trimmed hair. He smiled, moving his finger between her soft folds. She gave a long groan and willingly let her legs drop apart, inviting him to delve deeper. He took her lips in his. His erection throbbed with impatience but he was determined to take it slowly. Her body trembled under his touch as he teased her to the brink of release. Willingly she gave herself to him as a deep need to be possessed overwhelmed her. He slipped his fingers inside her moving them slowly, drawing her upward. Her body reached heights that she had never dared believe existed. Her head rocked from side to side as she gave into the intense sensations now racing through her body. Unable to stand it any longer she began plead with him to fill the desperate urgency growing inside her. Her hands glided down over his chest and abdomen tracing the lines of his hard taut muscles finally closing around his solid erection. He let out a tortured groan. Both of them were now desperate to have what they had both been trying so hard to avoid. She smiled, drawing her hand along his length. His body tensed with every stroke of her hand. He was now fighting to maintain control. As she flicked her tongue across his hardened nipples he let out a deep groan. He reached down, stilling her hand. Rolling her over on her back and with a hurried urgency he pushed her legs apart with his knee and entered her with a quick powerful thrust. She cried out, finally feeling the power and strength which up until now she had only dreamt about. Willingly she accepted everything he had to give, as he thrust into her time and time again. She raised her hips, meeting every one of his strokes, urging him deeper their bodies now moving in perfect harmony. His jaw clenched as another long groan escaped her lips and she felt herself slipping over the edge. Crying out his name she frantically clutched him, her body riding a wave of pure ecstasy. She felt him stiffen as he gripped her hips and thrust into her releasing himself deep inside her. They lay with their bodies still entwined, chests heaving raggedly. He remained inside her, reluctant to leave her feminine warmth. Finally he let out a long sigh and withdrew, rolling away from her. He lay back on the grass, still unable to believe that after all these years of waiting his dreams had finally come true. She was everything he had ever hoped for and more. Had he finally found what he had been searching for all these years? He rolled onto his side to face her, propping himself up on one elbow. Her eyes were closed. He tensed. She looked relaxed enough, and dare he say contented, and she had seemed willingly enough. Her body's rhythm had matched his perfectly, and those soft moans were enough to drive any man crazy. He could still feel where her fingernails had dug into his back. She sensed him looking at her and opened her eyes. There was no need for words the look in her eyes told him everything he needed to know. With a contented sigh she snuggled against him. It had never occurred to her that it could be like that between a man and a woman. He dropped back down on the grass, pulling her against him. She took comfort in the steady drumming of his heart. The tension of the past few weeks had finally left their bodies. Carley nuzzled against his neck making a contented little sound which warmed his heart. They stayed locked in each other's arms under the warmth of the afternoon sun.

Carley blinked her eyes against the sun. A smile touched her lips. Finally, she knew what it was like to make love and what it was that had been missing in her life. She felt as if nothing else mattered as long as she was with him. Draping her arm across his chest she began to playfully toy with his nipple. He stirred at her touch, instantly aware of her naked body pressed up against his. He opened his eyes to find her propped up on one elbow watching him.

He smiled "You okay?."

She nodded, as she moved her fingers across his chest in slow tantalising circles.

"I was just wondering, do you think there is any chance we might try that again" she said teasingly, almost sure after that marathon of love making he wouldn't yet be ready.

He grinned. "I think that could be arranged."

She raised her eyebrow in surprise.

"As I said before, I'm here to please."

She laughed. It was like music to his ears. He reached over and took her lips in his, feeling a little quiver run up the length of her body. She pressed herself against him.

He drew away momentarily and smiled at her "You know, if we carry on like this I can't be responsible for the outcome."

Her eyes glistened in the sunlight "1 was sort of counting on it."

He rolled his eyes "I can see it's going to be a full time job keeping you satisfied."

She giggled "But I'm so easily pleased."

He smiled drawing her into his arms. "Hmmm..., is that so?"

He stood up and drew her to her feet. Before she knew what was happening he had scooped her up into his arms and was heading towards the house carrying her as if she weighed nothing at all. He nearly dropped her when he tripped up the step. He gave her a cheeky grin as he quickly regained his footing. She reached back and slapped his bare backside.

"Ouch..., what was that for?"

She grinned "For nearly dropping me, for starters."

His eyes darkened. "Careful, pay back can be a dangerous game as you well know." he said, giving her a decidedly serious look.

An excited quiver to shot through her body "Bring it on."

He stepped through the front door "I hope you're ready for this."

She smiled. "I'm more than ready."

He gave a little groan and headed for the bedroom. Walking up to the side of bed he threw her down on it. He had often dreamt of her being in his bed, her tanned skin now a stark contrast to the pale cream sheets.

He liked how her long hair cascaded down over his pillow.

Her eyes travelled his body. She bit down on her lip. He stood with no shame at his obvious arousal. Her eyes took in his strong, muscular form, knowing only too well that she would again submit his needs..., and hers. She had never realised that you could actually want someone so badly.

She let out a squeal as he leapt onto the bed nearly bouncing her off the other side as his body landed heavily next to hers. Her hands gripped at the sheets as she tried to avoid falling on the floor. He took hold of her, drawing her against him. She could feel the hungry urgency as he pressed his lips firmly down onto hers. She responded eagerly, grabbing him, pulling him on top of her as her legs spread to accommodate him. The sound of his low raspy breathing and the feel of his heart pounding in his chest had her wet with wanting. Her body was ready and willing to accommodate him as his engorged maleness began to seek her entrance. He pushed himself inside her, letting her warmth wrap around him. She let out a loud moan. He liked the fact that she seemed to need him as much as he needed her. Her legs wrapped around him feeling every one of his muscle tense as he drove himself into her without caution. Her hands gripped at the bed sheets, as he took what he wanted, driving himself into her time and time again. They danced the same dance; her moves matching his. Powerful emotions welled up inside her causing every one of her nerve endings to scream. Her body spiralled upward, teetering close to release.

Her fingers sank into his back as she let out a deep moan and slipped into one of the most powerful climaxes she had ever experienced in her life. Her thighs clutched around him drawing him deeper. He thrust into her letting out a long tortured groan as he again released himself inside her.

He could feel her wildly beating heart vibrating against her chest. So many times over the years he had dreamt of having her in his bed and making wild passionate love to her. He smiled. What they had just done had definitely been way beyond any dream he had ever had. She moved beneath him. He reluctantly withdrew, rolling off her onto his back. Pushing herself up on one elbow she looked down at him. He reached up and gently tucked her hair back behind her ear.

A smile played at the corners of her mouth, "hmm..., me Jane you Tarzan."

They both laughed.

She fluttered her eyelashes at him, "I suppose I should be thankful I didn't get thrown over your shoulder."

He grinned, "I hadn't thought of that, maybe next time."

"May...be" she said dreamily. A frown creased her brow. Was it possible that fate did exist and she did belong here after all?

He saw her frown. "I'm sorry, I..., hope I wasn't..., umm, you know, too rough. I should have...."

She lifted her finger and held it up to his lips silencing him, "it was..., fine..., honestly."

He raised an eyebrow "Fine, huh."

She drummed her finger against her lips, "Well actually..., if I was being honest. It was more like...," she grinned. "amazingly mind blowing."

He smiled drawing her into his arms "Now that's the answer I was searching for."

She rolled her eyes, and snuggled up against him.

About an hour later, hunger drove them to leave the comfort of the bed. Carley headed off for a shower while Dean drew on a pair of boxers and went out to the kitchen to get them something to eat. She emerged from the shower feeling refreshed. She could hear Dean out in the kitchen. Choosing the smallest towel she could find she wrapped it around her body. Looking in the mirror she shook out her hair, grinning at her scantily clad image. He turned when she entered the kitchen. His eyes instantly darkened and he let out a long groan as he hungrily took in her attire.

"Surely you could have found a bigger towel than that?"

She gave a twirl, giving him a glimpse of what lay beneath and smiled. "You don't like it?" The light danced in her eyes as they travelled the length of his body. Her lips turned up at the corners ever so slightly as her eyes locked with his.

His body tensed, "Ooh..., I like all right, but I think it might be safer for everyone concerned if you put some clothes on."

She grinned. "I don't seem to have any. They are still out by the lake." He made a move towards the door.

"No need, I'll go" she said dropping her towel to the floor and turning to make her way out towards the lake.

He walked to the kitchen doorway to watch her as she moved through the house and out onto the porch, her hips swaying seductively. A smile played on his lips; being with her was certainly going to be entertaining. He relaxed against the doorframe, thinking about all the lost years that they could have been together. With a shake of his head he pushed them away. She was here now, that was all that mattered. He didn't need to know, he tensed, if there had been other men in her life. He grinned as she bent to retrieve her clothes. Picking them up and flipping them over her shoulder she turned back towards the house. Taking her time she strolled back into the house stopping just short of him. Her eyes locked on his as she lifted her arms up and drew her fingers through her hair so it lay down her back. A sly smile touched his lips as she slowly began to dress. He shifted position feeling himself harden

"The way you are going you'll wear me out."

Wiggling her bare bottom as she drew her skirt up her legs, was nearly his undoing.

"That's the plan" she replied drawing up the zip. Next came the waistcoat, he watched her as she slowly did up the buttons.

"There, all done." She said brushing up against him as she passed through the doorway into the kitchen. "So what's to eat?" she glanced back over her shoulder. "I've worked up quite an appetite." Dean's eyes were drawn to where her skirt hugged the curves of her small toned buttocks and slim hips. He pushed away from the doorframe and walked over to the sofa; picking up her lacy underwear he tucked them in his pocket.

"It's not overly exciting I'm afraid, just left over's from lunch"

"Mmm..., sounds good to me. I've had more than enough excitement for one day." She said blinking her lashes at him.

He smiled "I think I might be inclined to agree with you. We wouldn't want to spoil you, now would we?"

Her fingers ran lightly down his bare chest she felt his body tense under her touch.

"A little spoiling now and again doesn't do anyone any harm."

He grinned, "Eat..., you need a little more beef on your bones. I'm sure you've lost weight. I don't like my woman skinny."

She smiled, "you don't huh, well I'll better make sure to eat then, hadn't I? But just so you know, it's not much fun eating alone."

"Well I'm sure we can remedy that. How about from now on you come out here and eat with me." His eyes darkened "and anything else that might take your fancy."

She fanned her face with her hand. "Well now sir, that's one mighty fine offer. How could a lady possibly refuse? There is one condition however."

He raised his eyebrows "Ooh, there is, is there, and what might that be?"

Her eyelashes fluttered. "If I do come out for dinner, I get to stay the night."

He held his hands up in front of him. "You won't get any argument from me." What she was suggesting was better than he had expected.

He would agree to anything right now, just to be with her. He smiled. "Can we shake on it, you know, to seal the deal?"

She reached up and lightly brushed her lips across his "Consider it signed sealed and delivered."

His eyes scanned her face. "You have just made me the happiest man alive."

She blushed. "Ditto, except for the man thing, but I have to say you are very easily pleased."

He grinned, "What can I say? I'm a man who likes the simple pleasures in life." He took her hand and led her out onto the balcony. "Now eat, you'll need your strength..., for later.

Chapter Nineteen

She couldn't believe that a month had passed already. Their relationship had become even more passionate and intense over the past few weeks, if that was at all possible. She hadn't realised that life could be so wonderful. Everything, if she dare say it, seemed perfect. After three weeks she had finally given into his subtle hints and abandoned her motel room to move in with him. Her house was now finished and ready for sale. Everything in it had gone to the homeless shelter. The few small items she had kept were now safely packed away in a suitcase in the spare room. Dean had arranged for all the contractors, most of whom he knew personally, to help finish the house. The painting and decorating was finished and the gardens were looking spectacular. He had also been good enough to clear out her old room for her.

A smile crept onto her lips as she strolled up the drive. Today she was meeting with the Estate Agent. Finally, after weeks of sweat and tears, she could finally put the house up for sale and with any luck rid herself of the last connection to her past. The sale would give her the chance to re-coop some of the money she had sunk into it. Her stomach tightened as she approached the house. A woman stood at the gate. She waved at Carley and it was obvious she already knew who she was.

"Hi" Carley called as she neared.

The woman walked up with her hand held out, "Hi, Carley isn't it?"

"That's me, hey, thanks for coming."

"My pleasure, my name is Sandra."

Carley took her hand and shook it "Hi Sandra, have you had a chance to look around."

"No I thought it best if I waited for you..., shall we?" she said pointing towards the front porch. They walked up the front steps together.

"So, what's the market like at the moment? Do you think I'll have any trouble selling it?"

"You shouldn't do. It looks great on the outside, and it is in a good street. Shall we go inside and have a look?"

"Sure'" Carley unlocked the door motioning for Sandra to enter. "Take your time, have a good look around. I'll wait out here if that's okay with you."

Sandra stepped through the door "That's fine," she replied as she disappeared inside.

Carley sighed, as she sat down on the step. She had seen enough of this damn house to last her a lifetime. All she wanted now was to get it sold. There was a time when she thought that doing it up like her mother had always wanted would have somehow helped her overcome the pain. It hadn't. Now she hated the house, and wanted to be rid of it as quickly as possible.

She rose to her feet as Sandra reappeared through the front door.

"So, what do you think?"

"Excellent from what I've seen. I'll just have a quick look around the back."

Carley followed her around, stopping at the edge of the house to watch as Sandra walked around the boundary.

"Very nice" she called back over her shoulder. Luckily, the grass had grown back and the burnt patch was no longer visible. The damaged shed had been cleared away and the contractors had trimmed all the trees and tidied the gardens. Carley face creased into a smile as she thought back to the day of the fire when she had first laid eyes on him. Sandra walked back over to her and Carley's thoughts quickly returned to the present.

"Well it all looks great and honestly, I don't think you will have any trouble selling it."

Carley smiled "That's what I wanted to hear and what about the price? How much do you think it might fetch?"

They walked back to the front gate. Sandra started searching through her handbag. "I'll have to go back to the office and check the prices of other properties in the area. I can get back to you tomorrow, if that's all right and we can decide on a price."

Carley nodded "Sure, no problem, whatever it takes."

Sandra looked up at her "Have you got a contact number I can call you on?"

"Sure" she recited her number as Sandra wrote it down on her pad. "Are you going to be living in the house?"

"No..., I'm not, I'm staying down in a cottage by the lake" Carley replied pointing in the direction of Dean's house.

"Ooh!" Sandra replied looking a little stunned "Dean's place?"

"That's the one."

"I..., I didn't realise that..., he."

Carley's eye's narrowed "that he what?"

Sandra looked away avoiding Carley's intense stare. "It's nothing forget

I said anything."

Carley sensed her discomfort. She asked again, her voice a little grittier this time "Look, if there's a problem..., I need to know."

"It's nothing honestly..., it's just..., Dean and I..."

Carley tensed, "Dean and you what?"

"Well, we were sort of seeing each other for a while."

Carley felt a sudden pang of jealousy "'Seeing' as in relationship seeing?"

Sandra nodded.

Carley's mood darkened. Why hadn't he told her? Now faced with it, she hated the thought of him being with another woman. A little hypocritical considering her past, but she couldn't help it. "So how long ago are we talking?" She asked taking the time to study the woman in front of her. Sandra was a beautiful looking woman, blonde hair, green eyes and smooth fair skin. She had a tidy little figure although she was a little shorter than Carley, but she was quite stunning. Carley felt a little intimidated by her, as she took in her expensive well tailored suit and perfectly styled hair. Her face was tastefully adorned with just enough makeup. The woman was obviously talented and a successful business woman to boot. Comparing herself to the woman in front of her Carley felt a little inadequate. What did she have to offer? She had no skills to speak of, well none she could openly talk about and she certainly didn't have any job prospects.

"So how long ago are we talking?"

Sandra hesitated "About four months."

"So what happened?"

Sandra fidgeted with the clasp on her case "Look I'm not entirely sure we should be discussing this under the circumstances. Let's just say he's a hard man to get a commitment from so I wish you luck in that aspect."

Carley heard the resentment in her voice. "How long had you been going together for?"

Sandra turned her eyes to Carley's. She could see the sadness in them. "Almost two years" she replied softly. "Now I'm sorry, but if you want to know more you'll have to ask Dean. It's not my place." Sandra started to move away, "I'll call you when I have a price sorted," she said as she headed towards her car.

"Great and thanks," Carley watched her go. So he had been dating and quite recently. She thought back to what Sandra had said and couldn't really understand it. As far as she could see he didn't have commitment issues, or did he? Was she making a mistake? Would she end up getting hurt like he had obviously hurt Sandra? Did he love her? He hadn't actually said it, but then neither had she. Were they both holding back, him with his commitment issues and her in fear of being hurt?

She glanced down at her watch. He would be home soon. A smile creased her lips as she tossed any thought of Sandra aside. It was sometimes hard for her to accept how truly happy she was. Finally she had the one thing she had always longed for, but had felt out of her reach. They had made love most nights and the most wonderful thing about that was that she got to fall asleep in his arms. Their lovemaking was always exciting and spontaneous, bordering on turbulent yet at other times it would be soft and tender. In the past, she would never have believed life could be so good. At times it almost felt too good. In the beginning she had expected it to all fall apart, but as time slipped by her barriers slowly began to break down. She felt safe with him like nothing could ever hurt her again. That was the part she was finding hard to accept. Her happiness now depended on him, and in the past she had always been let down by the males in her life.

She arrived back at the house in plenty of time to shower and change. The minutes slowly ticked by as she repeatedly checked the drive for his truck. With a deep sigh she wandered out to the lake edge. How idyllic her life now seemed. Her body tensed, it was almost too good to be true. Over the past couple of weeks she had been feeling a random uneasiness, a foreboding like something terrible was about to happen. In the back of her mind she knew that if the truth came out, everything could be taken away just as easily as it had been given. He had given her the life she had only ever dreamed of and what had she given him in return... nothing but lies. Tears trickled down her cheeks. How could she have ever thought she could hide her past? There was no way she could risk telling him now, the opportunity had long since passed. A light drizzle began to fall but she was so preoccupied with her thoughts she failed to notice. Her heart clenched. Was it wrong of her to accept his love? She wrapped her arms around herself. Was it too much to ask of him?

Dean pulled up in front of the house and turned off the ignition. His brow creased when he saw she wasn't waiting on the porch for him. He stepped out of the truck. His body stiffened when he spied her at the edge of the lake. Like her, he had been waiting for it to all fall apart. At times she seemed distant and troubled. He had tried to get her to talk about it but whatever it was, she obviously wasn't ready to share it with him. His heart rate quickened. She looked so vulnerable standing there all alone. The strong need to protect her washed over him. Yet somehow, her vulnerability made her look all the more desirable to him. He couldn't help but notice how her wet dress clung enticingly to her body hinting at her nakedness beneath. He closed the truck door quietly so as not to disturb her. The rain had eased but the temperature had turned decidedly cool. He approached slowly. Why was she out here in the rain?

She startled when she heard him approaching. All her insecurities instantly vanished the moment she looked into his eyes. He had given her the strength she had needed to deal with her past. "What on earth are you doing out here?"

She smiled dropping her hands to her sides, thankful that it had been raining so that at least now he wouldn't see that she had been crying. Her body gave a quick little shiver.

"Waiting for you." She needed him to make everything all right again to push away the dark thoughts of the past. His eyes travelled her body. Her wet dress clung invitingly against her curves. He moved closer and smiled when he heard her sharp intake of breath. He brushed the back of his hand across her peaked nipples which were now clearly visible through the wet fabric. He hardened, pulling her against him. His hands ran down over her buttocks. A small moan escaped her lips as he held her against him, his erection pressing impatiently into her abdomen. She wrapped her arms around his neck needing the warmth and security. The throbbing in his groin intensified as she willingly surrendered herself to him. His hands travelled her body with a sudden urgency. He needed reassurance that she was still his. Taking a good firm grip of her buttocks he ground himself against her. Her hands pulled at his shirt tearing at the buttons. His body tensed as her cool skin met with the warmth of his. Yanking his shirt off she tossed it to the ground. Her tongue sought his small peaked nipples, and she nipped at them playfully between her teeth. He drew in a sharp ragged breath as her fingers released the button on the waistband of his jeans. She slowly began to draw down the zip. Her hand slipped inside his jeans. He felt hot and hard as she released him from the confines of his clothing. He let out another long groan as her hands expertly drew him to the brink of control. He pushed her dress up her thighs, hoisting it up over her hips. His fingers slipped between her legs, delving into her soft moist folds. A moan escaped her as he lowered his lips to hers. His fingers continued to work their magic drawing her upward.

"Ooh... please..., she moaned, struggling against his grip.

He held her firmly. Her body was now quivering with wanting. He slipped his fingers from inside her and grabbed hold of the thin fabric of her dress and tore it open. Her eyes widened as she arched herself towards him. Grasping her around the waist he lifted her off her feet. Her arms slipped around his neck and her thighs instinctively wrapped around his waist. He took a few steps forward. She let out a little yelp as her back came up against the trunk of a nearby tree. Gripping her thighs tighter she secured herself against him. His engorged manhood was already nudging at her entrance. He pressed his body against hers wedging her firmly between the hard trunk of the tree and his muscular frame. She let out a small whimper as the bark dug into the soft flesh of her back, heightening her feeling of vulnerability. He entered her in one swift powerful thrust, driving himself into her with little regard to her comfort. Waves of ecstasy tore through her body as she felt the intensity of his need. The bark of the tree pressed painfully into her skin. Now lost in the moment, she was at his mercy and he had no intention of showing her any. He continued to thrust into her as she gripped tightly, riding him. Her thighs tensed with every powerful stoke. She called out his name as her body convulsed into a deep spiralling climax. A feeling of pure unadulterated pleasure rocketed through her body. He let out a long deep groan, his body tensed. He gripped her buttocks firmly holding her against him as he drove into her again and again filling her with his seed.

She clung to him, her body spent. Slowly he relaxed his grip and his breathing eased. Tears began to trickle down her cheeks. He glanced down at her and almost dropped her.

"Carley. I didn't mean... to hurt you."

She gave him a shy smile, "You didn't..., apart from a few little cuts and a bit of bruising,"

His eyes widened, "what!"

"From the bark.. on the tree..." she felt him relax. "I'm fine..."

He raised an eyebrow.

"Actually..., I'm more than fine" she looked up at him through half closed dreamy lids. The corners of her mouth turned up seductively

"What was not to like?"

"Jezzus... woman don't do that to me." He lowered his lips to hers. Sex with Carley was always exciting and passionate and he loved every minute of it. She was like a drug to him and he was well and truly addicted. He released her lips and leaned down to whisper in her ear. "You know Carley, I've never wanted a woman the way I want you, I just can't seem to get enough of you."

She smiled "Ditto... except a man not a woman" Finally she was ridding herself of all her past demons and it was all because of him. She put her lips to his and kissed him long and hard. Slowly they slid to the ground. Contented, she nestled against his chest. He rested his back against the tree. Both of them happy to be wrapped in each other's arms as they sat watching the sun slowly slip below the horizon.

He felt her give a little shiver "You know, as much as I like being here with you, a man's got to eat and I'm sure you must be getting a little cold."

She gave him a contented little smile. "Hmm..., well..., I suppose..., we should make a move.

You do need to eat..., to keep up your strength."

He kissed her forehead "For what, may I ask?" He slid his arm from around her and stood up to refasten his jeans.

She looked up at him coyly "I have a few things in mind."

"I'm sure you do," he replied reaching down and gently pulling her to her feet. What remained of her dress fell to the ground. Slipping his arm around her waist he guided her towards the house. Together they walked towards the bedroom. He stopped at the door and lifted his robe off the hook and placed it around her. Her bottom lip pushed out as he guided her arms up the sleeves.

"All in good time baby" he said laying a soft kiss on her forehead. She giggled when her hands didn't appear through the end of the sleeves. He rolled them back for her, then tied the tie firmly around her waist. The robe engulfed her slender frame.

"Hmm, very sexy" she teased.

He bent down and kissed her lightly on the lips, "You look damn sexy no matter what you are wearing. Nothing is certainly better. but I can live with this." A naughty twinkle appeared in his eye "For now." Taking hold of her hand he led her from the room.

They worked side by side preparing the evening meal. She didn't know her way around a kitchen. Most of her meals had been eaten in restaurants or through room service. He turned to her. "You can slice the carrots if you like."

She picked up a knife and waved it about in front of her. "Are you sure you trust me with this?"

He moved in behind her, taking her hands in his, guiding her as they sliced the carrots into thin strips.

"See, nothing to it."

They talked and laughed as the meal slowly began to take shape. She leant back against the counter and watched him work.

"By the way, I met someone today that you might know."

Dean looked across at her curiously "Who?"

"She says she knows you..., quite intimately."

His jaw tightened, his hand stilled. She bit down on her lip as she tried to stifle a smile. His brow creased. There was only one woman she could mean. Was that why she had been standing out at the lake? Carley let a few seconds pass "What was her name again, umm...."

He tensed.

"Sandra, I think" she caught his eye "Yes that's it... San...dra."

The room fell silent as he looked away from her.

Carley's back stiffened. Maybe she did have cause to be jealous. "Dean..., do you care to explain?"

He glanced across at her, the uncertainty was now clearly visible his face.

She suddenly felt cruel. She smiled. "I'm just teasing. I know you only have eyes for me, and any way, when would you get the time or energy for another woman."

He narrowed his eyes. "That wasn't funny."

She grinned. "I thought it was."

"Oh you did, did you?" His eyes narrowed "Well I suppose it was my own fault. I should have come clean in the beginning."

Carley placed her hands on her hips "Yes you should have."

He grinned, "Well there is no time like the present."

Her body tensed. Did she really want to hear this? "Dean, its fine you don't...."

"Oh but I insist..., let's see..., we dated for nearly two years, but things just weren't working out. Granted, she's sexy..., talented..., successful..., and if my memory serves me correctly." He grinned. "she's great in bed and she has this amazing way of...." He quickly sidestepped, as a loaf of bread sailed past his head. He laughed. "Is that what I get for being honest? Now you know why I didn't tell you." He reached out and quickly gathered her into his arms before she had a chance to find something else to throw. She melted into his embrace. They both began to laugh. He leant forward and whispered into her ear. "Just for the record she wasn't all that great in bed... No more secrets..., I promise." Her heart clenched, knowing she couldn't promise the same."

Chapter Twenty

The next morning Dean walked into the kitchen and was surprised to find Carley making breakfast.

"Mmm..., something smells good." he said, walking up behind her and sliding his arms around her waist.

She leaned back against him "How does bacon and eggs sound? After last night's marathon I thought you might need a good hearty breakfast."

He bent down and kissed her on the top of the head "I don't suppose it has anything to do with the fact that this is the only thing you know how to cook?"

She dug her elbow in his ribs. "You're feisty this morning."

"You know, a man could easily get used to this. A cooked breakfast waiting for him in the morning and willing woman in his bed at night; what more could a man ask for?"

She glanced up at him. "Didn't I tell you the breakfast thing only happens on Sunday's? The rest of the week you're on your own, buddy."

"Well, that's gratitude for you. I make you my sex slave and you can't even make my breakfast in the morning."

Carley laughed "And all this time I thought it was you who was my sex slave, right there whenever I want you and always willing to please."

He grinned "Hmm.., that doesn't sound half bad when you say it like that. You want it almost every night anyway."

She giggled; he was right. When she had done it for a living, it had seemed like nothing but a means of survival. Now she enjoyed every minute of it. Her eyelashes gave a little flutter.

"What can I say..., I like what you do to me."

He let out a low growl "Ditto."

They moved out onto the veranda to eat their breakfast.

"By the way, I was thinking of having a barbeque; we could invite a few friends over. What do you think?" It'll give them a chance to get to know you and I'll finally get the opportunity to show you off."

Carley stiffened. She didn't need anybody else, she was perfectly happy as she was. "I'd rather not, if it's all the same to you. No one likes me Dean. We don't need them."

His eyebrows drew together causing a deep crease to form across his brow "Come on, Carley. If you are going to stay here you need to make the effort to get to know some of them. You can't hide down here forever."

Noticing the concerned look on his face, she caved in. "All right, you win, but please not too many. I can invite Nancy and Robert. At least then I'll have two friendly faces in the crowd."

Dean drew her into an embrace "It will be fine, I promise. They'll love you. Anyway some of the guys from the station will be there. You sort of know them."

Carley blew out a breath, "I suppose so..., okay but I'm warning you, this could all turn bad."

"It won't. They'll love you, trust me. You worry too much. I was thinking of this coming Sunday. We would have a week to prepare." Carley still wasn't sure, but if it meant that much to him she would do it. "If it all turns to crap and they hate me, you'll only have yourself to blame."

He smiled "It's a chance I'm willing to take.

For the next week Carley ran around making sure the house was tidy, the lawns were mowed and the gardens weeded. She had even forced herself to venture into town for a few supplies. Nancy was thrilled and accepted her invitation immediately. Carley was cheeky enough to invite Sandra. Since she was now her realtor, it only seemed right. She wondered what Dean's reaction would be when she arrived. It was a little mean, but if she was going to be uncomfortable, then so could he.

Sunday finally rolled around. Carley paced the lawn. She had been ready for hours. Dean walked over to her and wrapped his arms around her waist.

"Are you okay, Carl's? If you don't stop pacing, you're going to wear a track in the grass."

Carley snuggled back against him "It's the waiting. It's starting to do my head in."

He smiled. "What if I got you a glass of wine, would that help?"

She smiled "That would be great, thanks."

He headed off inside and left her to nervously pace the lawn. He came out carrying a glass of wine and a bottle of beer for himself. She gratefully took the glass from him and quickly downed its contents. He raised his eyebrows. "Maybe I should have bought out the bottle." Giving a little laugh, she handed him back the glass. "No..., but another glass would be nice, to help settle my nerves."

He had just returned with her second glass, when the first car came around the bend in the drive. He placed the glasses down on a nearby table and took her hand, "It's just one of the guys from the station." She breathed a relieved sigh. An old Ford station wagon pulled up and parked on the grass beside them. Dean gave her hand a gentle squeeze. Wing Nut grinned as he emerged from the car.

"Howdy all" he said, as he went to the back door and opened it. He leant in, and when he stood back up he was holding a small child in his arms.

Carley's heart clenched. It still hurt to see young children with their fathers. The front passenger door opened and after a little bit of effort, a heavily pregnant dark haired woman got out. She opened the back door and three more children piled out. They headed over to where Carley and Dean stood. Dean stepped forward and kissed the woman on the cheek.

"I think introductions might be in order. Everybody, this is Carley. Carley, this is Wing Nut or Grahame, whichever you prefer, whom you have already met and this is his lovely wife Amanda". He placed his hand on the oldest boy's shoulder "And this is Michael".

"Hello" Michael said shyly.

"Hello" replied Carley smiling.

"And this is Teresa and Millie; then over here we have their youngest, but not for long, David. Carley bent down and introduced herself to the children. "I bet you would all like to know where the tree house is". All the children nodded. "If you follow me I'll show you." Millie glanced up shyly, taking Carley's hand. She led them around the back of the house. It was nice having Millie's little hand resting in hers. It bought back memories of her father. Her eyes glazed as she recalled a time when she and her father had found a little hut whilst out walking in the bush. They had built a fire and roasted marshmallows on a stick. Lately she had been seeing her past in a different light. Tears threatened to fall. She quickly shook them away, as she led the children down the path beside the house. As they turned the corner, the tree house came into view. All the children squealed with delight. It wasn't just any tree house. Dean had built it himself with no cost spared. He had always wanted one as a child, so when he bought the place he had built one. It had a thick rope ladder, wooden shutters, a small balcony and of course a fireman's pole. Millie dropped Carley's hand and rushed off with her brother and sister. Carley smiled as she watched them clambering up into the tree house. Maybe one day it would be their children playing here. Her thoughts strayed. Could she really believe that's what her future held? She stayed for a few minutes caught in her idyllic dream world. Pulling her emotions back into check, she headed back to the party. As she re-joined the group, Amanda looked at her and smiled, silently mouthing the words "thank you". Carley smiled back.

Amanda certainly had her hands full with four children. Carley suddenly found herself feeling a little envious.

Carley's stomach did a nervous little flutter when another car arrived, but relaxed a little when she saw who was driving. She frowned as she recalled how insistent he had been with her on the main street only a week ago. They waited as he parked his car beside the station wagon and got out. His eyes zeroed in on Carley. He walked in a direct line straight up to her and pulled her into a hug, pressing himself against her. His hand slid down onto her backside. He gave it a firm squeeze as he placed his lips to hers, his tongue seeking an opening. She discreetly rammed her knuckles between his ribs. He stepped back giving her one of his easy lop sided grins.

"It's nice to see ya again, Carley."

Dean cleared his throat as a warning, one that Spider chose to ignore completely.

"You watch out for him Carley," Wing Nut warned, trying to lighten the mood. "He's one for the ladies he is, and his hands wander something awful."

Carley gave a forced little laugh "So I noticed. Don't worry. I am quite capable of looking after myself."

Spider grinned "Hmmm... I'm sure you are."

Carley dared a quick look across at Dean, and saw him glaring at Spider. Spider however, seemed oblivious to the cold stare he was receiving. Dean was about to say something when he was interrupted by the arrival of another car. It pulled up next to the others, the doors opened and Nancy and Robert got out. Carley rushed over giving Nancy a firm hug, suddenly realizing how much she had missed her. She thanked them both for coming and walked them over to the group. She went around each person introducing them, making sure to leave Dean until last.

"Dean, this is Nancy and Robert." Robert and Dean shook hands. Dean leant over and gave Nancy a peck on the cheek. Carley smiled when she saw Nancy's cheeks flush.

"We have heard so much about you. It's so nice to finally meet you" said Nancy still looking a little embarrassed.

Dean smiled, slipping his arm over Carley's shoulder. "Likewise..., I want to thank you for looking after my girl while she was staying with you. She thinks the world of you, you know."

Nancy flushed again, "It was my pleasure, she's like the daughter I never had."

Dean smiled. Carley was wrong, people did like her..., what was not to like? She is beautiful, kind, loving and honest, what more could a man ask for? Carley began to get a little anxious as more and more people began to arrive. He had promised to keep it small, yet every few minutes she found herself being introduced to somebody new. She was finding it hard to remember all their names. Dean walked up to her, followed by a young man and woman, and two children. He gave her an encouraging smile, "Carley, this is Glen and his wife Sophie. They run the greengrocer's in town." He gently pushed the two children forward "And this is Ethan and Carla"

Carley smiled nervously, "Hi."

Over the next hour, people kept getting placed in front of her. Names and faces began to blur together. There was Trevor and Alex, the gay couple who ran the local bookstore, Henry from the local garage, Alan, the convenience store owner and Abigail, apparently the only hair dresser in town. Amy and Paul owned the Hotel at the other end of town and Tanya the solo mother with four children whose husband had been killed in a car accident. There were school teachers, accountants, dog groomers. The list never seemed to stop. Towards the end of the night Carley had given up on trying to remember names. She smiled, suddenly realising that the only thing that mattered was that she was actually having a good time.

Spider had cornered her in the yard a couple of times throughout the night. The first time he pulled her into a hug and had tried to steal another kiss. Luckily she had managed to wiggle free. He was a little drunk and overly affectionate so she tried to make a point of staying out of his way. The second time he was a little more aggressive in his advances managing to make her feel very uncomfortable. Luckily Smiley had walked up and yanked hard on his ear causing him to yell out in pain. Spider had sulked off mumbling to himself. Smiley had given her a small smile then turned and walked off. She had starred after him realizing that she should not have been so quick to judge him. After that little incident Spider had made a point of keeping his distance. She was glad Dean hadn't seen it. The last thing she wanted was to cause trouble between Dean and his workmates.

Dean's discomfort was plain to see when he had walked over to greet Sandra. She had stiffened and drawn away when he tried to kiss her on the cheek. They had stood talking for a few minutes looking very uncomfortable in each other's company. Dean glanced over at Carley a couple times. She had simply smiled back. After a short time they moved apart. Dean walked over to her "You could have warned me." She smiled "What and spoil all my fun. It was payback for not telling me about her in the first place."

"I don't know what I'm going to do with you."

Her eyelashes fluttered "I have several very good suggestions."

His eyes darkened as he took hold of her arm and pulled her against him, locking her lips in a fierce passionate kiss. When he released her, she was out of breath.

"Don't tempt me." He growled softly in her ear. "I hear there is an empty tree house out the back."

Her eyes widened "You wouldn't, not with all these people around?"

He grinned. "Do you care to put it to the test?"

Her heart rate quickened, knowing he would. He kissed her lightly on the forehead "Don't worry, you're safe, for now..., go and mingle." She saluted. "Yes sir," she replied, turning back to the party. Carley noticed that Sandra and Dean made a point of not being in close proximity to each other for the rest of the night. Sandra seemed too busy working the crowd looking for new clients, and he simply didn't seem interested enough to bother.

As the night wore on people slowly began to leave. They had all seemed so nice, she hadn't expected that. She glanced over at Dean; maybe it had something to do with her being with him. Or had it all been her imagination; had she misinterpreted their interest in her for hostility? Maybe it was her giving off the wrong vibe? By the time it hit midnight there were only a few stragglers left, Spider being one of them, along with Evan and Rowdy and two other firemen and their partners. In some ways she envied Dean. They seemed more like his brothers than work mates and were such a good crowd of guys. She made her way over to the front steps, where they were all talking and laughing amongst themselves. As she approached, Dean scooted along the step to make room for her. She sat down and snuggled up against him. Her eyes turned up to his "I have to admit. You were right. It was a great night..., thank you."

He nuzzled her hair "You're welcome."

Carley looked around at the others. "Thank you all for coming." They all agreed it had been a great night and decided they should do it more often. Carley looked across at the two she had been introduced to earlier, "I'm really sorry but I've forgotten your names already. I've been introduced to so many people tonight I didn't have a hope of remembering them all."

The man closest to her smiled "They call me Piker."

She struggled not to laugh.

His eyes met hers "It's been great to finally meet you. Dean is very tight lipped about his personal life."

She looked up at Dean "Is he now?"

Dean shrugged his shoulders "What can I say? I like having you all to myself."

"I think I can live with that."

Her attention turned back to the others "If you don't mind me asking, why do they call you Piker?"

"Oh, it's nothing really, just that I don't always go along with their silly pranks."

She laughed. "I can understand that."

He smiled "This is my wife Kirstin. Kirstin this is Carley, the woman who finally captured Dean's heart."

Carley smiled. "It's nice to meet you Kirstin."

Piker seemed like a good sort. She had seen him a few times throughout the night joking around with the guys. He was lightly built with hazel eyes and fine blonde hair and a wide generous smile. His wife was fuller figured, with a long mane of rich copper curls, deep green eyes and a smile which matched her husband's.

The man next to him spoke. "I'm Slugger," he said extending his huge calloused hand. When she shook it she was surprised at how gentle his grip was "And this is me missus, Lilly."

Carley smiled "Hi Lilly."

Lilly looked like a child next to her husband's massive frame. Slugger was solidly built and wore his hair closely cropped to his head. He was surprisingly soft spoken for a big man. The words 'gentle giant' came to mind. "So tell me, why do they call you Slugger?"

"When we have softball games against other stations I always manage to hit a home run. Slug them way out field, hence the name."

She smiled and he smiled back. "We haven't lost a game yet," he said proudly.

"A good man to have on your team I'd say."

They all nodded in agreement. "Tell me does Dean have a nickname?" All the men laughed except for Dean. Spider slapped him on the shoulder. "We call him Pyro as in pyromaniac."

Dean looked at her and shrugged his shoulders.

Spider laughed. "Last summer he managed to set the barbeque on fire, nearly took out the whole station."

Carley burst out laughing. "No way." She looked across at him. He wasn't laughing. Carley threw her arms around him "So we took quite a risk letting you near the barbeque tonight?" She said placing a light kiss on his cheek.

He shrugged "What can I say, now you know all my secrets," he leant forward and kissed her firmly on the lips getting wolf whistles from the men around them. He smiled "Life's full of risk," he looked down at her his eyes darkening "As you well know."

Telling him about her father was certainly one risk she was glad she had taken. She snuggled up against him as he wrapped his arms around her and drew her against him. Carley's brow creased as thoughts drifted. What would her life have been like had she not met him again? He had shown her how to love again. She smiled. In the knowledge that there was no other place she would rather be than here wrapped in his arms.

Chapter Twenty One

A couple of weeks had passed since the barbeque and Carley was finding life could actually be wonderful. She now took regular trips into town, and to her surprise found most people friendly and chatty. At times she had to pinch herself just to make sure she wasn't dreaming. Her life now seemed so perfect. The feeling of dread had all but vanished and she began to feel as if nothing could ever hurt her again. Throughout Dean's working week they had slipped into a daily routine. They would get up in the morning and have breakfast together sometimes choosing to sit out beside the lake. On the warmer mornings they would go for an early swim together. After he had left for work Carley would busy herself with domestic chores, shopping and walks around town. She had even started having coffee in town with Nancy, or Amanda and once Lilly. Preparing his dinner and doing his laundry seemed to bring her a feeling of belonging, something she now realized she had always longed for. She was standing at the sink preparing the vegetables when she heard the sound of an approaching vehicle. Out of habit she glanced up at the clock, he was early today. Undoing her apron she rushed to the front door giving a quick glance at her reflection in the hall mirror. Satisfied, she stepped out onto to the front porch. Her body went rigid as her world suddenly came crashing down around her. She stood rooted to the spot as she watched a Red Porsche round the bend in the driveway. Her hand flew to her mouth when she realized it wasn't just any red Porsche. It was hers, or at least used to be. Her heart rate accelerated. She shook her head in disbelief. Why now when everything was going so well. Her fists clenched as her fear quickly turned to anger. The car came to an abrupt halt in front of the house, sending clouds of dust up into the air. She watched the dust drift away in the still summer air just like her idyllic life would if she didn't get him out of here before Dean got home. Her eyes flicked to the drive; she still had time. Gary opened the door. At six foot two he looked a little awkward getting out of the car. He straightened up giving her an ugly leer. Her spine prickled.

"Hi sweet cheeks" he said as he walked toward her.

She was finding it hard to grasp the reality of the situation. How dare he come here and ruin everything? "What the hell are you doing here!" she spat angrily. "Why don't you do both of us a favour, and get back in the car and go back the way you came?"

"Now what sort of greeting is that?" he replied deliberately running his eyes up and down the length of her body.

She gave an involuntary shiver under the cold scrutiny of his stare. A feeling of revulsion washed over her. His cold black eyes bored into hers. How could she have ever let this disgusting creature touch her? His once familiar facial features now seemed gaunt and harsh. He wore his hair closely shaved, exaggerating his narrow pointed head, jutting cheekbones and thin tightly drawn lips. The thought that she had let him touch her made bile rise in her throat. Her fists clenched and unclenched in quick succession.

"What do you want and how did you find me?" she asked through gritted teeth.

He gave a loud throaty laugh. "Well babe, if you didn't want me to find you should have refrained from using your credit card. Any simpleton knows that."

His eyes settled on hers, "I knew where you were the day after you left."

Her jaw tensed. "So why wait until now?"

He grinned. "I thought I'd give you a little time to come to your senses. I was a little hurt that you didn't even have the decency to say goodbye."

"You know as well as I do that you would never have let me go."

"But you chose to anyway."

He took a step toward her "You've had your fun, sweet cheeks, now it's time to go back to work."

She glanced towards the driveway. "I don't want that life anymore."

He gave a cynical laugh. "I don't give a shit what you want. There's money to be made, good money..., and you're going to make it for me. You were my best earner, and you skipped out on me. I had to deal with a lot of very unhappy customers who won't settle for anyone else but you."

He moved to the bottom of the stairs "And besides that babe, I've missed you."

Carley doubted he would have the ability to miss anybody; the money maybe, her no. He leant against the hand railing looking like someone who had no intention of leaving until he got what he wanted. A feeling of uncertainty began to grow inside her. Knowing he wasn't the type of person to take no for an answer.

"Well I'm afraid that's your problem because I'm not coming back! Ever!" she snapped struggling to hide her growing fear. How could she have let herself get mixed up with such an evil man?

His eyes narrowed. "Is that right? Well we will just have to see about that, won't we?"

Her stomach clenched "Please... just leave me alone."

Ignoring her plea, he began to climb the steps. "Well, well, I suppose you think you have the perfect little life here playing the little wifey with..., Dean."

Carley gasped.

He grinned, "Oh, I know all about him..., Sandra was very obliging. I found her at your parent's house putting up a For Sale sign. I see you are about to come into some money. Well at least you'll be able to pay back the money you stole from me to create this new little life of yours."

"It wasn't your money, it was mine" she replied, tears now beginning to well up in her eyes.

He gave an exasperated sigh "Oh! Don't go and start blubbering for Christ sake" he snapped. "It's simple maths. My clients, my money, so pay up now, or get in the car."

Anger welled up inside her, and the fact that Dean was going to be home any minute wasn't helping. "I earned that money fair and square. It wasn't you who had to sleep with all those men" She tapped her chest. "It was me. When I left I didn't take anything that didn't belong to me" tears flooded her cheeks as she nodded her head towards the car.

He grinned. He liked his women vulnerable and Carley's pleas were already starting to arouse him. "What about the lost earnings I've had to sustain? Some of my clients have left because of you, and that's not even counting the bookings I already had lined up for you." He got to the top of the steps.

Instinctively she took a couple steps backwards as she looked around for a means of escape. "Well, how much do you think I owe you?" she asked trying to buy some time. She thought about running inside but she didn't have a key for the door. He would soon push his way in. He leered at her, "let's say thirty grand."

"What! I...I... don't have that sort of money..., when I sell the house I can give it to you," she stammered.

He ran his tongue over his lips. She shivered, suddenly feeling very exposed in her skimpy shorts and thin, barely there, top. He grinned, advancing on her. Taking a quick step back, she felt her back come up against the wall of the house.

He moved closer. "What if I don't want to wait?"

Carley's heart began to hammer away in her chest.

He grinned. "I've really missed you. Maybe since I like you so much I might consider waiting for the money, if I could have a down payment."

She tensed. "I don't have any money on me."

He grabbed her arm. "Well that's a problem." He moved closer. His warm breath brushed across her face. He smelt of alcohol and stale cigarettes. Gripping her arm tighter, he pressed his body up against hers. Her body went rigid as his erection pressed against her hip. Panic began to set in. She began to struggle. He lifted his arm and placed it across her throat, using his weight to hold it firmly against her windpipe. The more she struggled the harder he pressed. A feeling of light headedness began to wash over her. She stilled, knowing if she were to continue she would probably pass out. The pressure eased allowing her to take a quick gulp of air.

He grinned. "I like my woman scared."

Her eyes widened as he let out a deep throaty laugh then leaned in and forced his lips down on hers. She cried out as he nipped her lip between his teeth, drawing blood. It was obvious to her now that she was no match for him and had little option but to accept his advances. He forced his tongue inside her mouth. Her stomach contracted. She pushed down the urge to vomit, not wanting to anger him further. Finally he drew his lips away. His arm however remained firmly pressed against her throat.

"Brings back memories" he said, his spittle hitting her face. He slipped his free hand up inside her top and pushed it up to expose her breasts.

Her body began to shake as the reality of the situation hit home. He grinned, showing a row of brown stained teeth.

"Now that's more like it. I've missed these" he said, grabbing one in his hand and brutally squeezing it until she cried out in pain. He pinched her nipple between his fingers and twisted it painfully. Tears rolled down her cheeks. Every time she tried to struggle he put more pressure on her throat. Maybe if she struggled enough she would simply pass out. Then at least she wouldn't have to witness what he was about to do to her. As much as she wanted to, she couldn't bring herself to do it. Closing her eyes she tried to push past it telling herself that it didn't matter, that she had been here before, but deep down she knew that it did. Squeezing her eyes tightly shut she tried desperately to distance herself, to find that safe place, but it didn't work. It was no longer there. She let out a loud scream as his rough hands raked across the naked flesh of her abdomen. His hand moved the waistband of her shorts. Her struggles intensified but no matter how hard she fought, she knew in the end she was powerless to stop him. Another scream escaped her as he tore at the button securing her shorts. Her head snapped sideways as he struck her hard across the side of the face.

"Quiet, for fuck's sake woman, anyone would think you've never done this before."

Tears flooded down her cheeks, turning a watery red as they mixed with the blood now trickling from the side of her mouth and nose. She tried to block it all out, but she could still hear his ragged breathing in her ear. Finally he managed to release the zip on her shorts. Carley gave a small whimper as he tugged her shorts down over her hips and she felt them drop to the ground. She stifled a scream, pushing it deep down inside. Maybe this was no more than she deserved.

Before she even realized what had happened, Gary was wrenched away from her. Relief flooded over her, but very abruptly turned to shame when she saw Dean standing in front of her. Gary was struggling to stand as Dean gripped him by the collar of his shirt, nearly pulling him off his feet. Dean was yelling something at him but Carley was finding it hard to focus. She stood there paralyzed as humiliation and shame washed over her. Dean shook Gary violently from side to side.

"What the hell is going on here?"

Dean took his eyes off Gary and glanced over at her. His body tensed as he took in the nasty swelling already ballooning up on the side of her face. But it was her near naked form that pushed him over the edge. His restraint snapped as he turned on Gary, anger now consuming every part of him. He threw Gary down the front stairs. His fists balled as he followed him down. He grabbed Gary by the collar of his shirt and wrenched him to his feet. Carley heard the loud crack as Dean's fist connected with Gary's nose. Gary let out high pitched scream as he slumped to the ground clutching at his nose. Carley could see the blood already beginning to drip through his fingers. Gary pleaded for Dean to stop, but Dean was now way beyond any sort of control as he continued to strike blows at Gary's face and torso. Gary was no match for Dean's strength, or the anger that now consumed him. He lay crumpled on the ground as Dean pummelled him with one violent blow after another. Carley suddenly snapped out of her trance. She had never seen him like this before; if she didn't stop him it was likely Dean would kill him. Yanking her top back down and drawing her shorts up. She stumbled down the steps two at a time. Dean had Gary pinned to the ground, his fist raised above him. Gary was pleading for Dean to stop. Carley grabbed at Dean's shoulders and tried to pull him off.

"No. Dean, you've got to stop, you're going to kill him." She cried. "It's no less than he deserves," hissed Dean as he shook her off. She staggered backwards almost losing her footing. Dean's anger was preventing him from showing any sympathy for the man slumped on the ground in front of him. He raised his fist and thumped Gary again. "No" cried Carley rushing over again, this time taking hold of his arm.

He hesitated, his fist poised in mid air. He looked down at the man writhing on the ground, loathing what he saw. She was right. If he didn't stop now he could easily kill this man. A hard knot formed in his stomach. He had failed her again. His body shook with anger as he glared down at Gary. "Who are you?" He asked through gritted teeth as Gary lay there, whimpering.

Dean grabbed his shirt and shook him violently. "Answer me." Gary held his hands up in surrender "Please, no more" he pleaded. "I want answers" hissed Dean.

Carley caught Gary's eye over Dean's shoulder and shook her head slowly from side to side, silently pleading. Gary gave her an ugly lopsided grin due to the massive swelling already starting to appear on his face. "I know Carley. She used to work for me."

The colour drained from her face "No Gary, please..., not like this." Gary winced as he tried giving her another grin "Why Carley..., have you not told him yet?"

He said, shaking his head from side to side.

Dean brow creased as he looked from one to the other. "Will somebody tell me what the hell is going on here!" he yelled, still trying to control the anger coursing through him.

Gary looked up at him through puffy lids. "It's not really my place..., but if you insist. Carley here use to work for me."

Dean tensed, "I got that already."

"Well, she left owing me a lot of money."

Dean's eyes narrowed, "So you thought it gave you the right to come and do this?"

"Let me finish, this is where it gets good. Her clients weren't happy." Dean frowned, "Clients," his fist balled. "What damn clients, get to the bloody point before I hit you again."

Dean glanced up at Carley but she wouldn't meet his eye.

Gary gave a little laugh even though it hurt to do so "She is a hooker.

She gets paid a lot of money to have sex with very rich men."

She looked over at Gary pleadingly but he showed her no mercy. He told Dean everything about how she had made her living for the past twelve years, and that she had been his best earner and how men would line up just to be with her.

Carley slumped down on the dirt, feeling numb. Her new life was now gone forever, just as she had always suspected it would. She looked over at Dean but he wouldn't even look at her. She slowly rose to her feet and headed inside. Pulling her suitcase down she started to pack. Once it was full she closed it and went into the spare room to fetch the case which held her mother's things. When she reached the porch she still held on to the hope that he would at least give her the chance to explain. She needed him to understand that she hadn't had a choice, at least not in the beginning anyway. As she made her way down the steps she saw the Porsche weaving its way up the driveway. It surprised her that after that brutal beating he had received that he was still able to drive. Dean was standing at the lake edge looking out over the water. She started to walk towards him.

He held up his hand, halting her. "So, is it true?" he asked not bothering to turn around.

Her body tensed at the iciness of his tone. She stood silently not knowing how to answer. He turned to look at her. She could see the hurt in his eyes, but she knew the time had come to be honest. Hadn't she lied to him long enough? Tears began to trickle down her cheeks. "Yes, it is. All of it, but you need to..."

"I need to what...?" he gave a cynical laugh, "understand?" When he spoke she could hear the disgust in his voice. "Go, I never want to see you again," he spat, as he turned away from her.

"But Dean, please... I didn't...

"I don't want to hear it. Go...

She stood staring at him not wanting to believe that Dean of all people wanted nothing to do with her.

His fists balled as he spun on her. "Get out.... I can't stand the sight of you. Is that plain enough for you?"

Sobs began to rack her frame. Reluctantly she turned and began to make her way up the drive. As the distance between them increased, her hopes of him calling her back faded. She was alone again. Everyone she cared about always abandoned her eventually. Life without him was going to be unbearable, and it was all her fault. If only she had been honest in the first place when she hadn't had so much to lose.

Chapter Twenty Two

Dean turned to watch the woman he loved walk out of his life for the second time. His heart grew heavier with every step she took. The deep seated anger made it impossible for him to call her back. She had betrayed him in the worst possible way. His body shook with rage as his fists drew into tightly clenched balls. He had thought that he had finally found a woman he could spend the rest of his life with. His stomach contracted as he thought about all the men she had been with. He had all too willing, given her his heart and what had she done with it? Ripped it out of his chest and stomped all over it. The urge to go after her was fierce but he held back, unsure if he could ever think of her the same way again. The hardest thing about it was that he still couldn't see his life without her in it.

Carley stumbled up the drive dragging both her suitcases

behind her, wanting nothing more than to drop to the ground, shrivel up and die. She shuddered remembering the disgust she had heard in his voice. The very reason she hadn't told him in the first place. Her hand brushed away her tears. She could no longer find comfort in his arms. A new flood of tears streamed down her already swollen face. What was the point of trying to create a new life? She turned toward her parent's house. It was the last place she felt like being, but it was the only place she had left. The decision to leave had already been made. There was no way she could stay, not now. The thought of knowing that she would never again see love in his eyes tore at her heart. It was a look she had grown to know and trust. Her heart clenched. She loved him. There would be no changing that, which was why she knew she couldn't stay.

When she reached the house, she dragged her cases up onto the porch. Feeling along the doorframe she found the key. She hesitated momentarily, a cold shiver running up her spine. It felt like she was right back where she had started. Placing the key into the lock, she turned it and the door swung open. Her heart clenched as she looked into the empty house. Had it been waiting here for her all this time knowing that her life would eventually take a wrong turn? She slammed the door shut and took a quick step backwards. There was no way she could go in there, not now, not ever.

After a couple of minutes, her heart rate began to settle. She glanced down at the cases at her feet. Was this what her life amounted to? Two lousy suit cases and a house she could no longer enter. The tears had simply dried up, just like her heart as she tried to steal herself against the hurt. She slowly descended the steps wondering what she was going to do. Aimlessly she wandered around to the back of the property, stopping at the corner of the house. Her eyes scanned the yard, remembering back to a time when she had truly felt happy. An image of her on the new swing that her parents had bought her, sprung to the forefront of her mind. Her mother used to grab her by the ankles every time the swing swung towards her; it used to make her laugh. Carley shook her head. Why was life so unfair? How was it that some people got everything they desired, while others only suffered? She walked over to the back steps and slumped down onto the cold hard, unforgiving concrete. Her mind wandered back to the first time she had seen him. He had looked so irresistible. She shivered, remembering how it had felt the first time he touched her. With a deep sigh she pushed the thoughts away. What was the point in torturing herself, she was never going to feel that again. The sooner she accepted that the better off she'd be. The sun slowly began to drop below the horizon, but she was so lost in her own thoughts that she didn't even notice. Her head dropped against the wall of house, her mind now in a whirlpool of hurt and confusion.

Dean spent most of the night sitting out by the lake. He couldn't bring himself to go inside to bed. A bed they had spent many a long night making love in. He already missed the feel of her curled up next to him and wasn't sure if he was ever going to be able to move on from this. He used to think that he couldn't live without her and that no other woman would do, but now he just felt confused and hurt. The anger had slowly subsided, and by the early hours of the morning had been replaced with an empty ache. He began to think that maybe he could forgive her for her choice of lifestyle, but it was the deception that hurt him the most. How was he supposed to have protected her when she didn't trust him enough to tell him the truth? What sort of relationship would they have had? He glanced up at the rising sun. His stomach clenched. They had sat here so many times watching the sunrise together. Why had he sent her away? His brow creased. He leapt to his feet. He had promised himself he would protect her always and at the first sign of trouble he had sent her away. His body tensed. Hadn't she already been through enough? Guilt bit at him. He hadn't even given her a chance to explain. Didn't she at the very least deserve that?

Carley woke, feeling stiff and shivering with cold. A hint of daylight showed in the sky above. She stood up and slowly stretched her aching limbs. There were no more tears. All she felt now was a cold dark emptiness growing inside her. Maybe she just wasn't meant to be happy. Her future now seemed bleak, as she teetered on the edge of a big black gaping hole of nothingness. How could she go on without him? She shuddered. As hard as it was, she needed to somehow move on and get past this. The constant presence of the house loomed behind her. She wrapped her arms around herself, trying to ward off the chill that had settled around her heart. Tensing, she turned to look back at the house. All this time it had been here anchoring her to the past. A constant reminder of the pain she had suffered. There was only one way she could put an end to it.

She made her way around to the front of the house. As she climbed the front steps she saw her cases sitting propped up against the side of the house. She rubbed her forehead, unable to remember leaving them there. Her thoughts clouded as her mind played over the previous day's events. Confusion closed around her. It had all happened so fast, from the moment Gary turned up, the fight and finally Dean sending her away. Her body gave an involuntary shiver. The only clear memory she had was the look of disgust on his face. Taking a deep sobering breath she turned the knob and the door opened. A cold chill wrapped itself around her. This house held her past forever locked in its walls. Clenching her jaw she stepped inside. A single tear ran down her cheek and dripped to the floor. The sun was just beginning to appear above the horizon, but it did little to ease the fear she had locked away inside her. She shuddered as her thoughts turned back to what had been one of the scariest times of her life. Her hand gripped the door knob; she could feel his hands on her. The light in her room had been her last hope. If he would have only looked a little harder, maybe he would see that she wasn't her mother. He would enter the room and immediately switch off the light. She grew to believe that bad things happen in the dark, and to this day she couldn't be alone in the dark without it triggering a panic attack. The wooden boards beneath her feet creaked under her weight as she made her way into the house. She froze, her breath catching in her throat. Reaching out she switched on the hall light. She let out her breath. Quickly making her way to the laundry, she opened the cupboard under the sink and pulled out some of the old newspapers she had stored there for packing. Her hand closed over the box of matches which she had thrown in there after the fire. She grabbed them and hurried back along the passage through the lounge to the stairs. Could she do this? She reached out and gripped the banister, her eyes travelling up the stairs to the landing above. Why had she even bothered to fix it up? What had she hoped to achieve? A small cynical laugh escaped her lips. To end the torture? Well, that certainly hadn't happened. She was now right back where she had started. Alone and scared and standing in a house she didn't want to be in. Her shoulders tensed. How could her own father have betrayed her in this way? "FUCK the lot of them," she cursed.

Her bedroom door crashed back against the wall. Drawing in a deep breath she entered the room making her way over to the window. She threw the paper down on the window seat and pulled off a couple sheets of paper and began screwing in up into tight balls which she piled together on the floor. Gripping the new curtains she had so carefully chosen from the store, she yanked down hard. The plastic hooks gave way and it fell to the floor. She did the same to the next one, then scooped them both up and dumped them on top of the screwed up paper. A sudden gasp escaped her lips as a cold shiver ran up her spine. Her fingers fumbled in her pocket for the box of matches. Sliding it open she plucked out a match and struck it. Her fingers trembled as she held the burning match out in front of her. "Just drop it." she muttered to herself. The blackened stick dropped to the floor beside her. With shaking fingers she took out another one and struck it. She held the match up she watched as the flame slowly consumed the stick. Again the spent stick dropped to the floor. Frustrated, she tossed the match box across the room. What was wrong with her, she couldn't even do this right. Turning, she fled from the room and didn't stop until her feet reached the wooden boards on the front porch. In a blind panic she snatched her cases from the porch and headed out onto the street. She stood for a minute glancing up and down the street, unsure of which direction to take. Finally she turned towards the cemetery. So caught up in her own pain she didn't notice the Red Porsche parked across the street from the house.

Gary sat in the car, watching her make her way up the street. He thought about following her and giving her a little payback but he was in way too much pain. He pressed his hand against his ribs and flinched as a sharp stab shot through his chest. He was pretty sure one of his ribs was cracked. He glanced in the rear view mirror, noticing the unusual twist to his normally straight nose. Her boyfriend could certainly pack a punch. He grinned, correction, ex-boyfriend. He had made a mistake and hadn't timed it quite right which had resulted in a beating, but he would get even one way or another. He watched as she slowly made her way up the street, dragging her suitcases behind her. What a pathetic sight. At least he got a little satisfaction knowing he had ruined the idyllic little life she had created for herself. She disappeared over the rise. He turned his attention back to the house. His brow creased when he noticed the front door standing open. He had spent most of the night waiting in his car but he must have fallen asleep, because he hadn't seen her arrive. Originally he had intended on forcing her to go back with him and make her pay for what her boyfriend had done to him, but decided it was a pointless exercise. He had been about to leave when he had seen her rush out of the house. Holding his hand against his ribs he struggled out of the car. His eyes scanned the empty street as he slowly he made his way over to the front gate. He took a minute to rest under the tree in the front yard, away from prying eyes. Clamping his hand firmly against his ribs he started towards the house, his eyes constantly searching the street. It was a struggle for him to climb the front steps. A series of small groans escaped his lips as he navigated his way up them. He couldn't risk anyone seeing him. He would draw far too much attention with his swollen eyes, twisted nose and his badly split lip. With a bit of effort he finally made it up to the porch and ducked through the open door. His body slumped against the wall as his eyes scanned the room "Very nice," he muttered to himself.

Perspiration trickled down his face. Every step he took was sheer agony, but it had all been worth it. He opened the car door and manoeuvred himself in behind the wheel. He turned to look at the house, his hands gripping the steering wheel tightly. A grin spread across his face as the first signs of smoke began to appear from under the roofline. That would certainly teach her a lesson. Let's see her get her money now. He turned the key in the ignition and the car roared into life. Spinning the wheels he turned the car around and shot off down the road. He looked back through his rear view mirror and laughed. The sky was already filling with thick plumes of smoke. He would have liked to have stayed and watch it burn to the ground, but he couldn't risk being seen. She had made it so easy for him; all he had to do was strike a match and drop it.

When Carley got to the cemetery she deliberately walked the long way around to her mother's grave so as to avoid her father's fresh one. Tears were already trickling down her cheeks by the time she dropped down on the grass in front of her mother's grave. She brushed her hand across the headstone to clean off some of the moss obscuring her mother's name. "Hi mum," she said suddenly feeling awkward. "I'm sorry about the house. I don't know what came over me." She fell silent. Her fingers began to pick at the grass. "I have made it look really nice I think you would like it." She hesitated hoping for some sign that her mother was actually there but only silence stretched before her. Absently she began plucking at the weeds that had sprung up around the base of the headstone. She glanced across at the cases she had dropped at the edge of the grave. Taking hold of one she dragged it towards her. With shaking fingers she snapped the clasp open. The small wooden jewellery box that belonged to her mother caught her eye. Sitting back on her ankles she placed the box in her lap and carefully opened the lid. Lifting out the first piece of jewellery she held it up to sun, trying to visualise the last time she had seen her mother wearing it. It was a delicate gold chain with half a heart hanging from it. She touched her throat knowing she no longer wore the other half, having lost it years ago. Placing it carefully on the grass beside her she pulled out the next piece, doing so repeatedly until the box was empty. A frown creased her brow as she noticed a small yellow envelope pressed into the bottom of the box. She eased it out, instantly recognizing her name scrawled across the front of it in her father's untidy handwriting. She had looked in this box several times over the past few months and had never noticed it there.

Minutes ticked by as she sat there staring down at the envelope resting in her hand. She thought about simply tossing it away. Curiosity finally got the better of her. Flipping open the flap on the envelope she pulled out the piece of paper inside and unfolded it. A lump caught in her throat as her eyes drifted across the page. Blinking, she fought to hold back the tears.

My dearest Carley,

I am so sorry.... I have wronged you in the worst possible way. Believe me when I say I never meant to hurt you. I realise now I should have got help, for the both of us. I was so torn up with grief and I missed your mother terribly and didn't know how to move past it. You were like her in so many ways. I can honestly say I didn't know what I was doing. I know that is no excuse for what I did to you and I don't expect you to ever forgive me. I just want you to be able to move past this. I don't want your hatred for me and what I did to you, define who you are. You deserve better than that. By now, you probably know that I took my own life. I'm sorry for that, but I couldn't live with the guilt and the shame any longer. Every day I wished I had handled things differently. If I could have taken it all back I would have. So please try and put your past behind you and don't let the hurt I caused you eat into your soul, as it did mine. I let both you and your mother down and for that I will never forgive myself.

Love always.   Your Father

Still unable to digest the words she sat motionless staring down at the letter with glazed eyes. By the time she did eventually stumble to her feet, her legs were numb. She stamped her legs up and down, to get the circulation to return. Glancing up at the sun she tried to get an idea as to how long she had been sitting there. Her eyes turned back to her mother's grave.

"Goodbye Mum. I probably won't be back, just so you know. I love you." Tears trickled down her cheeks as she bent down and placed everything back into the suitcase and closed the lid. Stuffing the note into her pocket, she reached down and grabbed the handles of the suitcases. With one last look at her mother's grave, she turned and walked away, this time taking the path that would lead her up past her father's grave. As she approached the freshly turned earth her pace slowed, she drew to a stop in front of it. Dropping her suitcases to the ground, she stood staring down at the mound of dirt. Her thoughts turned back to the letter. Her fists balled. What right did he have to tell her not to let it destroy her life? How could he possibly have any idea how it felt to have your own father do those despicable things to you? A hard knot formed in her stomach as she thought about what she had had to do, just to survive. She stood for a long time, just staring down at his grave, feeling nothing but hatred coursing through her body.

Maybe if she had realised how much he had suffered, she would have thought differently. He had hated himself for not having had the strength to stop. On that first night when he had visited her room he had come home to an empty bed. His life had seemed so meaningless and he had felt so alone. He had only meant to go in and hold her and tell her he loved her, like he used to when she was little. When he entered her room she had woken and in his tortured mind when she had looked up at him, with her hair all tussled and that sleepy look in her eyes, he had seen his wife. It was a look he had become so accustomed to seeing when he had regularly arrived home late from the night shift at work. He had reached for her needing comfort, and before he knew it, he was doing things to her that he had had no intention of doing. The black hole he had been living in for the past couple years disappeared and his wife was again by his side. She had given him temporary relief from his pain. Regrettably, he had been unaware that he was inflicting more pain on his daughter than he had ever experienced in his life. When she ran away, the reality of what he had done became clear. He was a broken man, not worthy of life. He had lived daily with the heavy burden and knew there was no forgiveness for what he had done. He had destroyed his daughter's life and had taken away her innocence.

She pulled the letter out of her pocket and tore it up, throwing the pieces down onto her father's grave. He was right, she would never forgive him. Turning from the grave, she picked up her cases and slowly walked away. A quick glance over in the direction of the lake made a fresh wave of tears flood her cheeks. Was she destined to always be alone? She stopped at the public toilets to get changed and wash her face, tidying herself up best she could. The swelling was still quite visible and a deep angry bruise was starting to appear on her left cheek. She flinched as she dabbed at her swollen nose. Giving a hysterical little laugh she turned from the mirror. There was no way she would be able to get by on her looks now, at least not for a while anyway. She sighed. Leaving the toilets she headed towards the bus station.

Chapter Twenty Three

Dean flew up the drive, dust curling out behind his truck. He had spent the night thinking about everything that had happened and had come to the conclusion that he had let her down again. What a coward he had been, sending her away like that. His male ego had certainly got the better of him. Recklessly he pulled out onto the road, almost collecting the letterbox. "Shit," he cursed as he planted his foot on the gas and fish tailed it up the road. His eyes were drawn to a large plume of thick black smoke billowing up into the sky. Easing off the gas he momentarily considered going to the station to see what was up, then just as quickly changed his mind. There were more important things to deal with and besides that, it was his day off.

His breath caught in his throat as he turned into Edgewood Drive and saw the smoke encasing her house. A sudden thought flashed through his mind. Had she been upset enough to?..... He shook his head. No she wouldn't... would she? He planted his foot on the accelerator, shooting up the road at breakneck speed. His truck jumped the curb as he jammed his foot on the brake, stalling the engine. It came to a screeching halt with its bumper resting up against the tree. He flung open the door, almost falling on the ground in his rush to get out and sprinted towards the house. His eyes searched the road desperately hoping to see the fire truck rounding the bend. The street remained empty apart from the few people who had gathered to watch. Looking back at the house he knew time was of the essence. The air was already thick with smoke and the flames were now beginning to make their way across the roof.

"Carley!" he yelled as he ran up the front steps. There was no answer. "Carley!" he yelled, even louder this time. Still there was no reply. If he waited much longer it would be too late, if it wasn't already. He knew he only had seconds to act. He glanced up the road; what was taking them so damn long? What he was about to do went against everything he had ever been taught, but he needed to know for sure. He kicked open the front door. The sudden burst of air caused the fire at the far end of the hallway to intensify. His body tensed. Maybe it was already too late. Pulling his shirt up over his mouth he cautiously made his way towards the stairs. It looked as if the fire had started upstairs so if she was anywhere he guessed it would be there. Forgetting that he wasn't wearing gloves he reached out and grasped the brass handrail. He cursed, snatching his hand away as an intense burning seared through his skin. Fighting the pain he moved on. As he climbed the stairs the heat intensified, burning the back of his throat. He could hear the sirens wailing in the distance. The house was already full with dense black smoke. There was no way he was going to lose her. He would never be able to live with himself if something had happened to her because of his stubborn stupidity. The further up the stairs he got, the less he could see. With one hand out in front of him, he felt his way to the top of the landing then dropped down onto his knees. The rooms at the end of the hall were already well alight. He placed his hand on the first door he came to. It wasn't hot, so pushing it open he crawled in. The thick smoke closed in behind him.

Carley walked into the bus station and made her way directly to the counter where she purchased a ticket to San Francisco. As she handed over her money she was aware of the woman staring at her. Snatching her ticket off the counter she walked over to the seat to wait. A cold numbness settled over her as she thought about the life she was heading back to. A life, which only months ago she had been desperate to leave. After everything that had happened, would she even be able to do it anymore? Her shoulders slumped. What was the point of trying to carve out new life for herself when the one she really wanted didn't want her? A small pang of guilt hit her when she thought about what she had nearly done. Her head dropped back against the wall. Burning the house down wouldn't have solved anything, except to rob her of her hard earned cash and put all her friends in danger. She glanced down at her watch, it was at least another hour before her bus arrived. It had been a long walk to the cemetery and back and she hadn't exactly slept all that well last night. The thought about heading off to get a coffee crossed her mind but before she could even bring herself to move she drifted off to sleep.

Carley gave a startled gasp when someone reached down and gently shook her shoulder.
"Excuse me, but I think that might be your bus."
Carley blinked sleepily. A young blonde haired girl stood in front of her, she pointed to the ticket booth. "That lady over there said I should wake you."
"Oh, right..., thanks." Carley stretched and went to rise.
The girl remained where she was, staring down at her. "What happened

to your face?" She asked inquisitively.

Carley flinched as a sharp twinge of pain shot through her cheek. "I walked into a door" she replied as she rose to her feet. Picking up both her cases, she headed toward the bus. The young girl stood staring after her.

A short queue had formed as the passengers waited for the driver to take their cases and place them into the luggage compartment. Two young girls stood ahead of her, chatting to one another. Carley's couldn't help overhearing their conversation. Her eyes widened when she heard them mention a house fire. Her heart skipped a beat, surely it couldn't be? What if the house had caught fire after all? She hadn't even bothered to check that the matches had gone out. Her stomach clenched.

"Excuse me, but did you just say there was a fire?"

Both girls turned to glare at her, annoyed at the interruption. Carley saw the surprise on their faces when they saw her injuries. They glanced at each other then back at her.

"It burnt to the ground apparently," replied one of them stiffly. "Where did you say it was?" she asked reluctantly. Already knowing what the answer would be.

One of the girls gave a long sigh, "Edge something, I think," she replied.

Carley spun on her heels, dragging her suitcases behind her as she hurriedly made her way back to the ticket booth.

"Hi, look I'm sorry, but an emergency's come up and I can't go. I was wondering if you had somewhere I could store my cases?"

"You know we don't do refunds?"

Carley nodded. "Fine, I don't care. I just need somewhere for these." She nodded to the cases at her feet.

"For twenty dollars I can give you a locker. For every extra day it's two dollars" replied the woman. Carley pushed her money through the grate. The woman passed her back the key, then pointed over towards the row of lockers "They are over there, number's on the key."

Carley snatched up the key and quickly hauled her suitcases over to the locker. Turning the key, she opened the door and tossed her cases in. After ensuring it was securely locked, she placed the key in her pocket sprinted off.

The smell of charred timber assaulted her nostrils first. Her hopes died. So, on top of everything else she had now managed to burn down her own house. She stopped at the gate to look at the remains of what used to be her family home. Her eyes moistened. What had she done? She gulped back the tears as she took in the devastation before her. With that one stupid act she had lost it all. The house was now just a large pile of burnt timber and twisted roofing iron. How could she have let this happen? Tears filled her eyes when she noticed the front door lying discarded on the front lawn, its surface burnt and blistered. The chimney now stood as a solitary reminder of the house that once was. There were odd bits and pieces that hadn't been completely destroyed by the flames, scattered around the yard. A small piece of the stair banister, part of a window frame with its paint still intact. They looked like lost pieces to a jigsaw puzzle. The tree in the front yard stood as strong as ever despite the slight curling of its leaves on one side. With the house gone it now dominated the desolate scene. The post box also remained untouched by the day's drama.

Chapter Twenty Four

Carley nearly jumped out of her skin when someone touched her lightly on the shoulder. Spinning around she was surprised to see Sandra standing beside her.

"Such a shame," Sandra said softly. "I actually had someone interested in buying it, you know."

Carley didn't reply as her attention returned to the burnt remains. Sandra placed her hand on her arm. "Are you okay? It's all a bit of a shock, I know."

Carley drew her arm away.

"Carley, these things happen, it's not your fault."

She turned to look at Sandra. Tears began to spill down her cheeks. "Isn't it, some would say otherwise."

Sandra's brow creased, "I don't understand, they say it was arson."

Carley gave her a forced smile "And they would be right."

Sandra smiled reassuringly. "Look on the bright side At least he won't get away with it."

Carley turned to look at her. "He?"

"The lady next door said she saw some guy in a red Porsche hanging around. She took down his licence plate number."

Carley gave a strained laugh, thinking the car was probably still registered to her.

"Someone said they saw this guy go into the house, then after he left, they noticed the fire."

Carley stared blankly at her. Sandra shuffled her feet then looked back over at the remains.

"Anyway, I just came to get my sign before someone decides to damage it. It looks like you won't be needing it now."

Carley looked back at the house "No I don't suppose I will" she replied, biting back the tears.

"I'm sorry to hear about Dean. Is he okay?"

Carley froze "Dean! What about Dean?" she snapped, as a sudden feeling of dread blanketed her.

"Oh, umm, I thought...," she hesitated.

"Spit it out" Carley hissed.

"I don't know all the details but I heard that he was taken to hospital by ambulance earlier. They found him inside the house. I thought you knew."

Carley crumpled to the ground "Oh No! what have I done?" She had bought all this into his life. It was all her fault, every last bit of it. How could she have done this to him? Why couldn't she have just left him alone?

Sandra put a comforting hand on Carley's shoulder. "I'm truly sorry, I thought you knew."

Carley looked up at her "Where did they take him?"

"Down to the local hospital I think."

Carley leapt to her feet and started to run as she had never run before.

"Carley, I'm sure he's fi..." Sandra shook her head as she watched

Carley disappear up the street, "fine."

Carley headed in the direction of the Hospital, praying silently to herself that he would be okay. Her mind began to race through all the worst case scenarios. She pushed herself harder. Her lungs began to scream for air, but she wouldn't let up. She needed to know one way or the other.

Bursting though the front entrance of the Hospital she stumbled up to the front desk. Her breathing was coming in short sharp gasps, which made it impossible for her to speak. The woman behind the counter shook her head unable to understand a word Carley was trying to say. She needed to find him and tell him she was sorry..., for everything. The nurse came out from behind the counter and tried to get her to sit down.

"Please take a minute to settle down. Now, what was it I can help you with?"

Carley gave a few sharp gasps as she tried to catch her breath. She pulled away from the woman and fled up the corridor, startling the patients as she ran from room to room. By the time the nurse caught up with her she had already checked most of the rooms on that floor.The nurse grabbed her arm, halting her.

"You can't go running around upsetting all the patients." She took in the distraught look on Carley's face "Now let's see if I can't help you. Who are you looking for?"

Carley looked at her pleadingly "There was a fire, a man... he, he was bought..., here, I must find him," she said between sobs.

"Oh, I see," said the nurse. "Are you a relative?"

Carley gave a strangled sob, thinking the worst, as she reluctantly shook her head. Her shoulders slumped in defeat, "I... I... ju... just need to know He's not d...ead..., is he?" She stammered, her breathing now slowly returning to normal. She dropped her head into her hands "It's all my fault."

The nurse hesitated, "Dean..., is that who you're looking for?" Carley glanced up "Yes."

The nurse patted her shoulder "He's fine, honestly, he inhaled a little too much smoke and got a nasty burn on his hand but other than that he's fine. He was discharged about twenty minutes ago."

Carley heaved a sigh of relief as she slipped to the floor. The nurse crouched down beside her.

"Are you okay?"

Carley gave her a weak smile. "I am now. Thank you for telling me. If it's alright with you I'll just sit here for a minute or two."

The nurse nodded, getting to her feet. "As long as you are sure you're okay?"

"Honestly, I'll be fine."

The nurse smiled, then turned and walked back up the hall towards the front desk. Tears of relief began to trickle down Carley's cheeks. If they had released him, then he must be okay. She got to her feet and slowly walked out of the hospital and made her way back to what used to be her home.

When she got there, she flopped down in the shade under the tree and stared at the ruins. Why did everything in her life always have to turn to shit? She had come here with all good intentions and in only a few short weeks managed not only to make more of a mess, but alienate the only person she really cared about. Her body shivered as she realised how close she had come to getting him killed. Maybe this was how it was supposed to be. He was better off without her. Stepping away would be the right thing to do for everyone concerned. He deserved a chance at a normal life, without all the drama that seemed to follow her around. The only option open to her now was to leave and never return. Her brow creased, but first she had a promise to keep. Rising to her feet, she set off in the direction of the lake. She found herself thinking about the letter her father had written. Especially the part about how she shouldn't let what he had done to her destroy her life and that she deserved better. The words kept running over and over in her head on instant replay. She gave a little laugh. What did he know? He had opted for the easy way out. She squared her shoulders and tilted her chin up, knowing she was better than that. As she neared the lake the guilt began to creep in. She had willingly drawn Dean into her life and had very nearly got him killed. Her body tensed as the house slowly came into view. If she had any other choice she wouldn't have come, but she had made him a promise and she meant to keep it. Leaving him would break her heart, but it had to be done. It would be the best solution for both of them. Her step slowed as she neared the house. The front door was open and his truck was parked in the driveway. She took a deep breath and headed towards the door. The house stood in silence. Climbing the stairs she knocked on the open door. There was no response. She knocked again, louder this time. Still there was no response. Reluctantly she stepped inside and quickly checked the rooms; they were all empty. She moved back out onto the porch and glanced around at the deserted yard. Why did Gary have to go and spoil everything? She shook her head. Truth be told, the blame rested on her shoulders. If she had just been honest in the first place, then maybe none of this would have happened. A cold ache clenched at her heart. She had had the life she had always dreamed of, and she had let it slip through her fingers. How could she have been so stupid as to think she could keep her past a secret? If she had just given him a chance to understand she could have explained it to him properly, instead of him hearing it all from Gary's lips. It wasn't as if she had a choice, at least not in the beginning. It had been a matter of survival and she had hated every second of it. The stillness surrounded her; her brow creased. Maybe she wasn't going to be able to keep her promise after all. Giving a long defeated sigh, she headed up the drive. There was no point in torturing herself any longer. The sooner she could put this all behind her, the better.

She gave a startled gasp when he suddenly appeared from around the corner. Her eyes widened as she took a couple of clumsy backward steps. He stood rigid, the expression on his face impassive and impossible to read. Her heart rate quickened as it did every time he was near. Even now, after everything that had happened she could feel the need for him growing inside her. Her body gave an involuntary little quiver as she stared up at him, unable to speak or draw her eyes away. She ran a quick critical eye over him checking for injuries. Her brow creased as her eyes came to rest on his bandaged hand. To her relief everything else seemed intact.

The deep seated anger that he had felt earlier had now returned with a vengeance. His eyes took in the bruising to her beautiful perfect face. Her lip was split and she had a nasty swelling across her right cheek, a stark reminder of her deception that had ultimately led to his failure to protect her. He noticed her looking at his bandaged hand. "It's fine, no thanks to you" he said coldly.

Only hours before he had wanted nothing more than to hold her in his arms again. Now the opportunity was here he couldn't bring himself to do it. Was the damage she had caused irreparable? Physically he was fine but emotionally he felt like a train wreck. His workmates had had to drag him out of the house. He hadn't wanted to leave until he was sure she wasn't in there. Relief had washed over him when they had told him the house was empty, but his relief had quickly turned to rage. He could have been killed. His body remained motionless, his emotions drained. What had she come here for? Forgiveness, or was it simply to say goodbye? Could his heart bear the loss again? She had the ability to hurt him like no else could. He braced himself for the worst. His eyes narrowed.

"What are you doing here?"

She stood dumbstruck. Being this close to him had her head in a jumble.

He glared down at her, his eyes blazing "Don't you have anything to say?"

Still she stayed silent.

"I could have been killed, of all the stupid...," he hesitated, "I thought you were in there."

Tears spilled down her cheeks "I'm so sorry, for everything, it's all my fault, I know that" she sobbed.

"Damn right it is. He was still seething inside but the sight of her crying, tugged at his heart.

"You know you could have saved us all a lot of trouble if you had just been honest with me in the first place."

Her eyes turned to his, "I, I..., didn't..., I'm sorry..., okay I made a mistake."

"A mistake," he gave a little sarcastic laugh. "I don't consider purposely misleading me a mistake. You had every opportunity to tell me you use to be a whor..., hooker, so why didn't you?"

Her shoulders tensed. "I did try, if you remember. But you told me it didn't matter, that it could wait."

"I wasn't expecting that you would be keeping something like this from me. Any man would react exactly the same way I did, in my situation."

"In your situation, will you listen to yourself. Anyone would think it was you who had too..."

"Had to what, sleep with all those men? Go on say it, Carley."

Tears flooded her cheeks "You stand there, judging me when you have no idea what it was like for me."

"It couldn't have been all that bad. You kept at it for twelve years."

She slapped him hard across the face, "I thought you were different. Now I see you just as narrow minded as the rest of the people in this town," she yelled, now bordering on hysteria.

His eyes darkened. "What did you expect? You based our whole relationship on lies. Were you hoping that I would never find out?"

She swiped angrily at her tears "Do you really want to know why I didn't tell you? Well, do you?"

He shrugged his shoulders "It won't change anything."

"Well you're going to hear it anyway. I didn't tell you, because for once in my life I was happy. I felt after everything I've been through, I at least deserved that." Her shoulders slumped, her emotions now completely drained. She turned her tear stained face up to look at him, knowing it would be for the last time.

"You know what Dean? I can't do this. I came down here to check you were okay, and to say goodbye. There would be no point in me trying to explain myself. You have obviously already come to your own conclusions, so let's just leave it at that."

He looked down at her. He hadn't wanted this, but he couldn't seem to keep his emotions in check.

Her tear-laden lashes blinked slowly across her eyes. "I promised to tell you when I was leaving, so here I am. I think it's the best for both of us. Maybe you can put all this behind you and move on with your life. I haven't got the strength to do this and you don't want to hear it anyway."

"Fine, Carley do what you always do. Run and hide."

Tears began spilling down her cheeks. She hated him seeing her like this. If only she could be strong, but everything he said was true. It was her fault, every last bit of it.

"You're right, it is my fault. So do yourself a huge favour and forget about me. Go and find yourself some wonderful woman who will make you happy." She pushed past him and stalked off up the drive. "Goodbye Dean, have a nice life" she yelled over her shoulder, her heart aching more with every step she took. This was the last thing she wanted. To have him gone from her life forever, was still unthinkable. Knowing she loved him made it all the harder but in her heart she believed he deserved to be happy. Even though she had no idea how she was going to cope without him. She loved him with all her heart and always would. Each step she took was taking her further and further away from the life she had always dreamed of, with a man who had helped make her feel whole again.

A frightened yelp escaped her lips as she felt his fingers wrap around her wrist. Before she knew what was happening she had been swept off her feet, and thrown over his shoulder.

"What are you doing, put me down this instant." She demanded, trying to wiggle free. Emotionally she felt she couldn't hold it together much longer. He was just prolonging the inevitable and the sooner he realised that, the better. Her struggles became more urgent. "Please, there's no point to this..., put me down."

He didn't reply as he spun around and headed back down the drive towards the house.

She thumped her fists against his back, "Dean, this is ridiculous, please let me down." she cried, as she thrashed about trying to get free with very little success. His hand slapped down onto her backside as he fought to hold her in place. She was now bordering on hysteria. "Why are you doing this? Please..., just let me go."

"I can't do that."

"Can't, what do you mean can't. Of course you can. Just put me the hell down."

He grinned, "If you'll just be quiet for a minute, I'll try to explain," he said sounding a little amused.

She struggled harder "I don't need an explanation. I just want to be put down."

He smacked her backside hard. "Ouch! I warning you Dean, put me down, I mean it."

"Sorry, no can do."

"Why the hell not?"

"I'm taking your advice and damn good advice it was too" he replied laughing.

Carley stopped struggling. "My advice! I don't remember giving you any advice." She tried thinking back over everything she had said, but hanging upside down whilst being carried over someone's shoulder could be a little distracting to say the least.

"You know, the bit about me finding a woman that could make me happy."

Her struggles resumed, "And what the hell has that got to do with me?" she spat. This wasn't the time for silly games.

"I thought you should be the first to know that I've found her."

"What the heck are you going on about?"

He gave an exasperated sigh "You know the part about finding a woman that will make me happy? Well, I've found her." He gave a little laugh, "I have to admit though, she does have some anger issues and a very, dare I say it, colourful past but nothing that can't be sorted." She stopped struggling. "I love her you see. I can't live without her."

Her body went limp as she tried to absorb his words. "What did you just say?" She asked now, feeling totally confused.

He started from the beginning, "I said I had found..."

She slapped his back, "No, no..., not that, the last bit."

He was grinning broadly now, not that she could see it, "What? The bit where I said I was in love with her or to put it more clearly, with you?" By this time he had reached the house. Without stopping, he took the front steps two at a time and walked through the front door, kicking it closed behind him. Her struggles had ceased as she hung unceremoniously down his back. He carried her through the house towards the bedroom and threw her down on the bed. He stood looking down at her. She daren't speak. Had she heard correctly? He frowned "You do understand what I just said, don't you?"

She nodded, unable to believe that only minutes ago she was standing on the drive saying her final goodbyes. "I don't understand. I thought that you..."

"I was stupid. I can't live without you Carley. I need you in my life."

"But what about my past, doesn't that bother you?"

"I'd be lying if I said it didn't, but it's something I will have to learn to live with."

"Are you sure? I can't go into this if you still have concerns."

"Carley, do you always have to over think everything, can't we just be happy and take one day at a time?"

She smiled, "If you can, then so can I."

He gave a relieved sigh. "Now if it's alright with you I think we have some catching up to do. Are you up for it or would you prefer to wait until later?"

Smiling she grabbed the waistband of his jeans and pulled him down onto the bed beside her. "I think we could possibly fit some in now, and have a little left for later. What do you think?" she replied giving a wicked little laugh.

He lowered his lips to hers and kissed her deeply.

"Ouch" she cried.

He quickly released her lips, "Sorry, I forgot."

He brushed his fingers lightly over her injured lip "I should have been there to protect you."

"How were you supposed to protect me when I wasn't honest with you?"

She pulled him closer and whispered into his ear "By the way, I love you too."

He drew her into his arms "Now before we get started, are there any more surprises that you have in store for me?" He said smiling. Not that he really cared. He wanted her past, her present and her future, no questions asked.

"No I think that's about it, no more surprises." A naughty little smile spread across her lips. "Now can we get on with that making up thing you promised me?"

He hesitated "Before we do there's one more thing I need to clear up." Carley looked up at him, stunned into silence. "Carley, the love of my life, will you consider becoming my wife?"

Tears formed in her eyes, "What happened to us taking it one day at a time?"

"I know what I want, do you?"

"Of course I do and the answer is yes, yes, yes and yes again."

He smiled as he gently lowered his lips to hers. Tears sprang from her eyes as a familiar warm feeling began to grow deep down inside her. She was finally going to have her happily ever after, with the man of her dreams.

Chapter Twenty Five

Carley lay in her husband's arms. It gave her a strange sense of comfort watching him sleep. Her fingers traced the outline of his lips.

His eyes slowly opened, "Good morning Mrs Baxter."

Rolling closer she kissed him lightly on the lips. "Mr Baxter," she snuggled against him. "Are you awake enough for me run something by you? I would really like your opinion"

His eyes focused on hers "Sounds serious."

"It is. I've been thinking."

He gave a little groan. She slapped him on the chest. "I'm serious. I need to think about what I'm going to do with my life."

He smiled "Apart from being at my beck and call you mean, hmm..., do you think you will have the time or energy for anything else ?"

"I can't just swan around here all day waiting for you to get home from work."

He pulled himself up the bed until he was resting against the headboard, "Okay, I'm all ears."

Determined to be taken seriously she sat up beside him. He drew the sheet up over her. Her eyes met his. He smiled.

"It's a little distracting."

Clutching the sheet against her, she leant against his shoulder. "I've been thinking about the empty lot where the house used to be. Instead of selling it, what do you think about us rebuilding on it."

His brow creased, "You said you hated the place."

"I did, well the house anyway. But that's gone now. In a way Gary did me a huge favour." She felt him tense like he always did whenever she mentioned Gary's name. "We could use the insurance money."

"Why do we need another house when we have this one?"

Her hands ran down the smooth lines of his chest. "Not for us silly. I want to build a house for runaway teens. I could incorporate counselling services and classes so they could learn skills and get a decent job."

He remained silent. She looked up at him. "Well, what do you think? I'll need your help of course. You could be my project manager and oversee all the building work and deal with the contractors."

He kissed her softly on the forehead, "I think it's a great idea. So when do we get started?"

Dropping the sheet, she climbed on his lap and straddled him. "We could start right now if you want." She nipped his nipple between her teeth. "I really need to get the project manager on side. Maybe get a few perks thrown in."

He grinned. "And what about your husband, what does he think of this?"

She smiled. "He's all for it."

She slowly began to rotate her hips. A smile played on his lips. "You know what I think? I'm going to like this job," he grinned "And all the perks that go with it."

www.ingramcontent.com/pod-product-compliance
Lightning Source LLC
Chambersburg PA
CBHW020114180626
46812CB00006B/2596